Flash and the Swan

Flash and the Swan

Ann Brophy

tempo
books
GROSSET & DUNLAP
Publishers • New York

TO MY FAMILY
AND TO FLASH LLOYD

Contents

June

THE
BEGINNING OF
SUMMER

THE city's drowning, Madeline thought.

The rain hit sharply against the roof of the car and streamed down the windows in hazy patterns. It was the kind of rain that arrives with summer, steady and insistent, determined to wash away the muddy rites of spring. She was reminded of halyards clacking against masts, of boats rocking at anchor. The windshield wipers swept back and forth, revealing quick images of stop lights and umbrellas splashed and blurred together. Horns and sirens coughed and screamed.

"I can't leave it when it's drowning." Madeline wanted any excuse not to go. "Maybe we should stay in town this year," she suggested.

"It gets too hot in summer," her mother said, "and you'd miss the boats and the water."

"I could catch up on plays and museums and galleries and things like that," Madeline offered. "I never have enough time in the winter."

"Madeline"—her mother's voice was soft and understanding—"it will be all right. You'll see."

She turned to look at her mother, who was bent over the wheel, staring at the road ahead. Her mother looked so tired, and much older than she had looked last year at this time. Her usually neat hair, which she wrapped in a thick, rich swirl on the top of her head, had slipped down and was resting on the collar of her raincoat. Her hands, with long, slender fingers, were so free and expressive when they worked on canvas. Now they were gripping the wheel of the car, and they looked cramped and swollen with strain. But most of all there was a deep sadness in her mother's eyes. Madeline could see it even now, after all this time, and she felt it envelop the car, as they passed the rows and rows of brick and concrete buildings crowded together, pushing and almost forcing one another into the water that surrounded Manhattan.

Madeline loved her mother very much at this moment, and she wanted to tell her so. She wanted to tell her how much she admired her, how much she liked her paintings, how beautiful she was, and how much her father had loved her. She wanted to apologize for taking up so much of his time and for not loving them both the same. She wanted to tell her mother so many things, but she didn't know how. She had never talked to her mother, and she didn't know what to say. She felt very awkward.

"I wish I could help you drive, Mom," she said stiffly. "You must be so tired."

Her mother smiled. "Two more years and you'll have your license. Then you can do all the driving. Besides," her mother added, "you had the hardest job—all that running around, packing the car. I'm just sitting."

Madeline smiled back and touched her mother's arm. I did have a hard job, she thought. Not because of the weight of the suitcases or the problems with fitting all the boxes into the car, one on top of the other, or the trips in the elevator up and down from the apartment to the street; what made it so hard was doing it alone, without him to talk to and laugh with and make plans with for the summer.

Her father had always taken charge of moving them from the apartment in the city to the summer house every June. When Madeline's school was out for vacation, they would pack up and head for the old New England town of Southport, Connecticut, on Long Island Sound, where they had spent every summer since Madeline was a little girl.

Now, as she grew older, she appreciated the summers even more, and the contrast with city life became more valuable and more pronounced. The sounds and the smells were different. She loved the feeling of freedom and the thrill of watching a sailboat, bulging with wind, soar across the water. Even the taste of summer was different, seasoned as it was with the sharpness of salt water on her lips.

Some of her friends in Southport would tell her how much they envied her living in New York. "There's so much to do there," they would say. "And it's so *boring* here," they would add.

"I hope I never feel that way," she said out loud, not meaning to.

"Feel what way?" her mother asked matter-of-factly.

"Feel sad again," Madeline answered without thinking.

Her mother smiled with effort. "It's all part of growing up."

"That's what I mean," Madeline agreed.

"What's Flash doing?" her mother asked.

Madeline appreciated her mother changing the subject. She hadn't wanted to talk about growing up. It was all so complicated.

"Flash? I almost forgot about him! Isn't that awful?" Madeline suddenly smiled.

Flash was growing older too, she thought, but in a different way. He didn't do much any more but lie around and sniff at his food when she put it down every evening. Often he never ate it.

"You should make him eat, Mad," her mother would say. "Get a spoon and feed him like a baby," and Madeline did just that many times.

"You ought to get a new golden retriever," her cousin Charles would say. "Flash is tired, and you should let him go."

But Charles had never known Flash the way Madeline had, because Charles was around him only in the summertime. Flash had been Madeline's dog all the time for as long as she could remember. So she fed him with a spoon and moved a pillow into the kitchen when he was too tired to climb the stairs every night.

With plenty of time for lying around the apartment, sleeping in front of a fire, winter seemed to suit his lifestyle now. But when summer came and they moved to the summer house, life moved outdoors and Flash was left behind. With Madeline on the go, he had trouble following, especially when she jumped in and out of the waves on the beach. He couldn't even play hide-and-seek with the water splashes anymore.

He used to swim with Madeline every day on the other side of the sea wall. They would race each other out to the float, Flash always letting Madeline win so she could pull him up. Then, when Madeline threw his ball back into the water, they would swim home again. Now he had trouble climbing over the sea wall, and when he walked too near the waves, his feet seemed to feel very cold and he shivered. So he would lie down on the sand in the sun and go to sleep.

He was asleep now, stretched out on the back seat of the car. Madeline reached over and touched his head. He recognized Madeline's hand for, without opening his eyes, his tail moved in appreciation, and he made a most comfortable sound.

"I don't think Flash looks forward to summer any more," Madeline said.

"We'll get a smaller boat this year for the two of you," her mother said. "He'll like that."

Madeline thought of her Blue Jay at the Yacht Club, the boat she used in sailing class.

When Madeline and her father had bought the Blue Jay three years ago, the boat was named *Banana Peel*. She was an older boat from Long Island, and she had a fast record.

"She's slipped across many finish lines first," her father had noted, as he carefully checked her racing records. "She's a winner."

"I like her name," Madeline had said simply.

So *Banana Peel* had come to her third home, with such fleetmates as *Blueberry Pie, Black Shadow, Jabberwock,* and *Five Grand.* And her reputation followed her, as her competitors often did, across the finish line. But *Banana Peel* was not a boat for Flash and her.

"We'll find one that you and Flash can handle

fine. One you can keep right there at the summer house, just as we did the big boat."

Madeline and her mother had sold the big boat shortly after her father's death. It was a sloop that had gone for only one sail, one perfect sail at the end of last summer.

The boat had been delivered the evening before. It was a gift from her father to himself, Madeline, and Flash in celebration of his latest book. Her father was a writer of some reputation. He had just finished a book to critical raves. "Colossal!" "A masterpiece!" "A monumental triumph!" Those words appeared over and over again describing his latest and best work.

"You see," he had said to Madeline, "you really should look into ancient history as your college major. Obviously no one touches the subject any more. No competition!" Then he had laughed, and his joy had filled the room.

Her father was a seasonal man, and summer was his season. He loved the water and boats and being with his family. He also loved his work, but he would have liked to have done it holding a tiller instead of a pencil, facing a good southwest wind instead of the walls of his study. He never looked forward to closing the summer house and returning to work in the city.

Madeline's eyes filled with tears, and she squeezed them shut so her mother wouldn't notice.

The memory flooded back, as it had many times before. Each time, she hoped that it would become clear, that she could understand what had happened and accept it at last. But she found that each time she remembered she grew more angry, and she always cried.

Her father and she had decided to go sailing that late August day to herald the book and the boat and the summer's end. She and Flash had gone down to the Yacht Club to meet him. Her father already had the boat at the dock when they arrived, the loosened mainsail luffing aimlessly in the gentle breeze. The bright noon sun reflected in the water with shimmering silver dots.

"What a glorious day!" Madeline shouted to the sky.

Flash wiggled at her side, impatient for someone to help him onto the boat.

She looked at her father, tall and straight beside the mast. Although he was much older than her friends' fathers, he was still a strong man, with a softness that comes from caring. And he looked unusually well that day, she thought. "He can't be sick," she told herself. "He's not going to die. The doctors are all wrong." She felt relieved by her decision.

"Come aboard, my lady," her father said, as he bowed and extended his hand. "I hope the new vessel is to our lady's liking."

"Oh, Dad, she's wonderful—perfect—I love her!" Madeline blurted, trying to take in the entire boat at one glance.

"My lady forgot her escort."

Flash was making irritated noises, anxious to be noticed.

Madeline turned. "Oh, your highness, forgive me," she pleaded and placed her hands gently under his front legs to help him aboard.

Flash checked the boat out methodically, sniffing all over her thoroughly and wagging his tail in approval.

"She's the most beautiful boat in the whole world!" Madeline announced, and hugged them both.

At the mouth of the harbor the wind picked up. Her father cut the motor and handed Madeline the mainsheet.

"Now, My Lady, we shall put her to the test. We shall sail the seven seas!" He took his place at the wheel. "First stop—Sunken Island. I'm going to show you a miracle!"

Madeline held the stiff line lightly, jiggling it a few times to get the feel of the crisp sail. She was filled with anticipation.

"Watch out for the swans!" her father called. "Hang on to Flash!"

The swans had been around the beach all summer. There were over a dozen of them, and at low tide they would parade proudly back and forth in front of the houses and allow people to feed them scraps of bread. But at high tide, they floated out near the mouth of the harbor, and they were quite stubborn about giving right of way to any boat.

Madeline's mother had warned her to stay away from them. "Swans are strange. You don't know where they come from, and you don't know where they go. Their wings are very strong. They are truly a mystery."

"Flash will take care of us," Madeline answered.

Flash growled heroically.

Then she saw one swan apart from the rest. He was floating tall and stately near the grassy knoll.

"Look, Dad! Look at the big one! Over here—off starboard! He's huge!"

Her father lashed the helm with a short piece of line and joined her at the rail.

"He's new around here. Quite a handsome guy. It's a good thing your mother hasn't met that one."

Flash was at Madeline's side, growling softly as he fixed his eyes on the huge swan.

"See, I told you Flash would take care of us."

"Let's go," her father called, back at the wheel. "This is your captain speaking. Trim the mainsail. Here's the best wind we've had all summer!"

Madeline braced her foot against the seat and pulled hard on the mainsheet. The sail filled and the boat surged ahead.

Flash was in the stern, his eyes still fixed on the swan, who was following the boat now as they passed the buoys and left the beach behind.

"Crazy bird, go away!" laughed Madeline.

Suddenly, with enormous wings spread, the huge swan rose slowly into the air. The bright sun was lost behind it, and the boat was eclipsed in its shadow.

"Look at that!" she called to her father. "It's weird!"

Flash was barking as he stared at the sky, but his tail was wagging. Madeline felt chilled for an instant, and she shuddered, almost dropping the mainsheet. Her father paid no attention. In a moment the swan had disappeared.

The Sound was filled with Sunday sailors. Mast after mast saluted the sky while their bows attacked the waves. Madeline and her father tacked until they were clear of companions and had a free course. Then Madeline cleated the mainsheet and walked aft to her father's side at the wheel.

"She's fantastic! So easy to handle! So smooth!" she exclaimed. "For a boat this size, she's incredible!"

Her father was pleased. He valued Madeline's opinion on boats, for she had had a lot of experience in sailing. He had taught her himself, and she knew her subject well.

"I've decided to call her *The Great Lady,* in honor of you," he said, "if, of course *my* lady approves!"

Madeline kissed him suddenly. "I love you, Dad!" she said. Without thinking, she added, "Don't leave us."

Her father walked slowly to the rail. He didn't answer. Beyond him, Madeline watched some late afternoon fog gathering on the water, and a white apparition seemed to be moving in with it.

She squinted hard, trying to penetrate the fog to see what was out there. She hadn't noticed her father rush to the wheel and give it a violent turn.

All of a sudden the boat had lurched, and Madeline slid sideways to the rail. She reached the mainsheet cleat just in time, for the boat began to swamp. She quickly released the line, letting the boom swing free over the water. The boat stopped, and the mainsail hung limp above them.

"Hey, Dad, come on," Madeline called. She didn't know whether to laugh or to scold. "Give me the news—'stand by to jibe'—remember!"

Her father sat down by the wheel. He, too, seemed a little shaken. "It's late," was all he said, "too late for Sunken Island." Then they headed home.

The day had been perfect. Only the evening was wrong. Her father had died that night. The doctors had been right after all. The family had talked many times of what would happen when her father finally had to leave them. All about heaven and how his spirit would always watch over them after he was gone. All about how much he would always love them.

Madeline had heard it all, but she had trouble believing it. She had told him just that afternoon not to leave them. But he had left anyway. She couldn't believe it. He had never let her down before—not ever!

That night, after dinner, he and Flash had left for a last summer walk along the beach. It was dark, and the air was very still. Only the swans floating on top of the water interrupted the sweep of tiny waves across the moonlit horizon.

"Anyone coming?" her father had called from the sea wall. "Last chance this year!"

They found him on the beach a short while later. Flash was still beside him, growling softly and wagging his tail.

Madeline was angry. "It's not fair! Why did he walk out alone?" She would have gone with him if she had known. Instead she stayed behind to help her mother with the dishes. Why did he die like that? He should have waited!

It was her mother who told her that her father's life, at that moment, was complete, and it was time to move on. Her mother's eyes had filled with tears. She told Madeline that someday she would understand. But Madeline stood on the beach, stamping the sand in fury and throwing handful after handful of rocks at the water.

"Madeline." Her mother broke the silence. "We need toll money."

Madeline pulled herself to attention with a shudder. She opened her bag and handed a coin to her mother.

As the car stopped, Flash roused himself and stuck his head between them.

"No biscuits till we get there," Madeline told him, closing her bag. He licked her cheek and put his head on her shoulder.

Madeline pressed her lips together tightly to hold back the tears.

"Are you catching a cold, Mad?" her mother asked.

"No, Mom."

Her mother put her hand on Madeline's arm. "It's going to be all right," she promised. "Don't worry. We'll have a good summer."

The rain had almost stopped, and she noticed the beginnings of a rainbow in the clearing sky.

The next moment the car crossed the bridge, and the city was left behind.

THE VILLAGE

THE village of Southport was tucked in protective hills. "Ancient Rome had seven hills, and so do we," her father had said, but Madeline knew there were really only three. To the east was Sasco Hill, like a giant's foot set down on the shoreline, where once had echoed the musketry of colonial soldiers as they fired down at British ships—men of war—their decks crowded with invading redcoats. Beyond Sasco Hill was Long Island Sound, the Race, and the Atlantic Ocean. When Madeline was younger, her father had shown her charts of the Sound. "See," he had said, "the Sound is shaped liked a bottle, and here"—he pointed to the Race—"is the neck, where the ocean tide surges in and out and the currents are swift and deep."

To the west was Mill Hill, with its grand views of the Sound, and above Mill Hill, very high, stood Greenfield Hill—horse country, with estates and woods and streams. There the polo matches were played every Sunday, and glossy-coated hunters and jumpers vied monthly for blue satin ribbons. Spring came later there, because it was higher and colder. The dogwood trees, thousands of them— pink and white—bloomed two weeks later than they did along the shore. So did the forsythia. The leaves turned sooner, too, in autumn, to golds and reds and purples and oranges, in a massive confusion of color.

Two of Madeline's friends—Tory and Lee—lived on Greenfield Hill. They were sisters whose father was the president of a local bank. He and Madeline's father had been old friends—both business and personal. That Tory and Lee were twins had always astounded Madeline, because they were so very different. Tory was athletic, outgoing, and always happy, while Lee had always been shy and thoughtful. She would agree with anything Tory said. Madeline figured it was probably because Lee was twenty minutes younger than Tory, that she was subconciously taking the lead from her older sister. That was why she followed Tory around like one of the dogs their mother raised. Lee even looked liked a poodle, especially when her boat capsized and her hair went all frizzy.

When they had been children, Tory liked to

spend every day in the village, because there was always something going on; and, of course, Lee came along, too. Six of them had formed a secret club in Aunt Ede's basement, and Tory had been elected president, at once, by unanimous vote. There were many important things to accomplish on those long summer days, like finding the little gray cat for Mr. Ludlowe after it slipped out of his store window, washing counters for Mr. Robinson when his air-conditioner dripped, and delivering a small order for the grocery or hardware stores. But, most important of all, there was just sitting on the great, soft, mossy rocks by the boatyard and watching the boats glide in and out of the harbor, and being happy.

Greenfield Hill was a good place for Tory and Lee to go home to because Tory's happiness—like her horses—needed space to expand and Lee needed privacy to think. They would have felt confined in the village, with its manicured lawns and tended gardens, where once the famous Southport globe onion grew. Farmers had taken the onions in wagons down to the harbor and loaded them into the onion schooners that plied the Sound to New York City. Onions were a staple in the diet of European immigrants then teeming in the city. "In terms of tonnage, we were the biggest port between Boston and New York," her father had said. And it was true, but not now. The onion warehouses— solid, massive, whitewashed brick buildings—had decades ago been turned into Pequot Yacht Club, with gold cupolas and black iron weathervanes, polished oak floors, varnished cases of ships' models, and the colorful flags of other yacht clubs along the walls. And, at the end of the parking lot, was the heavy machinery—hoists and derricks and winches and ships' tools. The racing boats—Blue Jays, Lightnings, Lasers, and Fireballs—stood in rows on their boat trailers, like cadets at attention.

Whenever Madeline thought of the Yacht Club and the harbor, her image was of a blindingly sunlit summer day, when the American flag and the Yacht Club flag crackled and snapped in the breeze at the top of the flagpole. And she could hear the brass cannon, which boomed at sunrise and sunset as the flags were raised and lowered by the launchmen. The cannon glistened so brightly that it hurt her eyes to look at it.

The great "goldplaters"—sloops, yawls, and ketches thirty, forty, and fifty feet long—nestled in finger slips in front of the Yacht Club. "Grand dames at afternoon tea," her father once had said. Madeline loved their names—*Ariel, Far Horizons, Southern Cross, Wave Dancer, Spindrift, Cygnet, Edelweiss, Wild Hunter,* and last year, for only a short time, *The Great Lady.* These were yachts that had raced to Bermuda, Halifax, and Rio de Janeiro and cruised the Caribbean, the China Sea, the Indian Ocean, and the vast Atlantic. When the wind was high the water shivered with sparkles, and the yachts jostled in their slips merrily, remembering the taste of faraway seas. Their binnacle compasses gleamed, their varnished decks shone, and their hulls were the whitest white.

The summer days were long, and it seemed to Madeline that the sun grew tired staying up so late. Once it could touch the trees on the hilltops, it slid quickly down behind them and disappeared. But it always waved good-bye with the most glorious shades of pink and gold streaking after it.

Madeline missed those evenings all winter long. Now and then she might be able to catch a glimpse of a sunset between some buildings, but the beauty was always squeezed too thin. Madeline was glad that her mother was an artist. Her mother painted pictures all summer, so that all winter they could remember and enjoy the same beauty.

Southport was a village steeped in history and suspicious of change. Madeline's father had been an enthusiastic supporter of the Society for the Preservation of the Village. Even after he had grown up and moved to the city, he kept in close touch with Southport people who, like himself, were dedicated to keeping the village, as practicably as possible, the way it had been in the past. Whether it was her father's interest in history or his appreciation for lasting beauty, Madeline couldn't decide. It was probably a lot of both. Her father had admired strength, and his village had been strong.

"You've got to hand it to us Connecticut

Yankees," he had said with pride. "No British soldier was going to drive us out." And although those British soldiers had marched stoically and systematically through Southport, torches in hand, they could not destroy every family or burn down every house.

Aunt Ede's house was one that had survived the Revolution, proud and tall, lording it over their summer house and all the rest of the newer houses along the water. She and her brother, Madeline's father, had been raised there, in that house, opening and closing doors so swollen with age they no longer fit their molded frames, and walking on wide, creaking maple floorboards that sagged from generations of pounding feet. The house had seven fireplaces and two chimneys, and it had been added onto three times. The last time was nine years ago, when Aunt Ede's only grandchildren, Charles and Lisa, started spending their summers with her. Their father, Michael, was an important executive with an international business concern. Charles and Lisa had been born in France, and the family lived in a house just outside Paris. Every year, since they were little children, they had spent their summers with their grandmother in the house in Southport. The children and Aunt Ede loved the arrangement, and their parents were delighted because it gave their children a sense of roots and them a sense of freedom.

That same year, nine years ago, Madeline's father had decided to build a summer house in front of Aunt Ede's on the strip of land by the water, the same land where the old barn had once housed the horses and stored the onions. The British soldiers had burned the barn to the ground.

"A little girl has to have a place to run and play and be in the sunshine. And Flash would like it better, too," her father had said to her mother. "A little girl and her dog shouldn't be cooped up in an apartment all year." And Madeline's mother, being from California, had agreed.

"Let's stop at the market and pick up a few things now." Madeline's mother broke her reverie. "Then we won't have to bother Aunt Ede for breakfast tomorrow." She parked the car beside Hebert's Market. The village was quiet that afternoon, and there were very few cars. Madeline guessed that everyone was rushing the season down on the beaches.

"Nothing's changed," her mother remarked, glancing around. She reached into her purse for a comb and repinned her hair into a neat swirl on top of her head. She is so beautiful, Madeline thought. No wonder Dad loved her. Madeline wished she could have looked like her mother, with rich dark hair and full cheeks the color of pale strawberry taffy and dark-brown eyes that were already made up naturally. Instead, tall and gaunt, with deep-set blue eyes and sculptured cheekbones, Madeline favored her father's side of the family. She would look exactly like Aunt Ede when she grew up.

"If you want anything at the drugstore, Mad, why don't you run on over there now."

"Okay." Madeline got out of the car and stretched. It was a long ride from the city, and she was stiff and tired of sitting.

The village was laid out in a triangle. "Three corners, not four," her father had said. "Yankee thriftiness." Hebert's Market was at the apex. The other corners held Robinson's Pharmacy and Bartlett's Insurance Company. Each narrow, winding road led off from the corners like a tentacle from a giant octopus. There was a lunch place next to the pharmacy with a neat wooden sign hanging on a brace. It read simply, A SANDWICH SHOP, and in small letters underneath, the word "pizza" had been added to entice the younger trade. Next to the insurance office, the hardware and marine store displayed brightly colored wheelbarrows and barebecue grills along the sidewalk. Anchors were propped up beside the door.

Down the street was the small brick post office with peony bushes hugging the mailboxes, and beside the post office there was an old-fashioned country store with a cat asleep in the window. Outside, newspapers were piled high, waiting for the paperboys. Madeline had helped Charles with his paper route one summer, and they had made over five dollars a week, including tips.

The country store was called The Candy Kitchen by the children. Filled with all kinds of candy, it was the most popular place in the whole village, and the most profitable.

Madeline noticed the signs in the grocery window: COLD SODA—35¢ and LET US STOCK YOUR BOAT FOR YOU. "Soda's up," she said matter-of-factly.

Flash had put his paws on the back of the seat, his huge head sticking through the window and his tail wagging in fast circles.

"Well," Madeline said, patting his leg, "you *are* glad to be back, aren't you?" Flash barked. "Okay, wait here and I'll be right back. We'll be home in a few minutes." Flash sat back down dutifully.

Madeline loosened the rubber band that held her ponytail together and let her hair hang free in long blonde waves down her back. After running her fingers through it a couple of times, she crossed the street to the drugstore. She was glad to see that Mr. Robinson had filled the window boxes with geraniums this year. Last year he had tried petunias, which by the middle of summer were incurably straggly.

"Hi, Madeline! Welcome home!" Mr. Robinson called from behind the counter. "Glad to see you back this summer!" It was still obvious that Mr.

Robinson had been a star football player in high school—a long time ago—even if he was balding a little now and his once rugged shoulders stooped a bit. He was busy unpacking a box of combs and setting up a display next to the magazine rack. "You're quite the young lady now. You've gotten all tall and beautiful. Just like Mrs. Robinson says—the city is full of gorgeous models."

Madeline was embarrassed. "Thank you, Mr. Robinson," was all she could say.

"Mrs. Robinson and I were afraid all winter that maybe your house would be empty this summer. We wouldn't have liked that. No, we wouldn't have liked that at all." He handed her a comb. "A welcome home present."

"Oh, thank you, Mr. Robinson."

"It wouldn't be the same around here without you folks," he went on. The ancient overhead fan revolved quietly. Madeline felt very warm as she fingered the toothbrushes, wishing that Mr. Robinson would stop talking. She knew what he was going to say. "We really thought your dad was extra special. You know, even after he became so famous and wrote all those great books, he was still just the same as he was in our high school days. It was so sad last summer when he—"

"Thank you, Mr. Robinson," Madeline broke in.

"Yes, sir, we were real happy when your aunt asked us to unlock the shutters and get the house ready."

"Thank you." Madeline handed him a toothbrush across the counter.

"You're good folks to come back. I know it must be hard, but I know he's happy you did. He loved his summer house."

Madeline shook her head in agreement. Her throat felt tight, and she swallowed hard. "Thank you, Mr. Robinson," she repeated again, as she took the paper bag. He must think I'm an idiot, a real broken record, Madeline thought, walking toward the door. Thank you, thank you, thank you, Mr. Robinson. But what else could I say?

"That's the most polite little girl ever to come to this town," she heard Mr. Robinson remark to a man at the counter.

The flag outside the grocery store was fluttering briskly above the village notice box. Madeline crossed over to look at the posted bulletins. A good day for sailing, she thought to herself. I guess Mom's right. I *would* miss the boats and the water.

"Hi, Madeline!" a husky voice called from behind her.

Mrs. Davis waved enthusiastically as she waddled across the street from Bartlett's Insurance office, where she was the secretary. Madeline liked Mrs. Davis. She had always handled her father's insurance without a complaint, and Madeline well remembered how difficult her father could be when it came to anything that had to do with his boats.

"You look great!" Mrs. Davis bellowed, beaching

herself at Madeline's side. She was an extremely heavy woman with a very happy face. She smiled broadly now, and the corner of her mouth twitched in rhythm with a dangling yellow curl bouncing on her forehead. "You know, honey, *The Great Lady* is back!"

"Here?" Madeline winced.

"Some man at the club—new this winter—bought her and sailed her down from Maine just last week."

Madeline tried to smile, but she felt her own mouth twitch once or twice. She never wanted to see *The Great Lady* again. "Is she moored in the harbor?" Madeline asked, hoping she wasn't.

"She sure is." Then Mrs. Davis, realizing Madeline's dismay added quickly, "But she's not dockside like before. She's farther down. You know, his being new to the club and all, he doesn't have priority."

Madeline was relieved. At least she wouldn't have to see *The Great Lady* every time she went to sailing class.

Mrs. Davis gave Madeline a hug. "I hope I can help you again this year, my dear. I really loved that dad of yours."

Madeline squeezed her hand.

"Love to your mom." She walked away, blowing a kiss.

She's really a good-looking woman, Madeline thought. She always wears the latest style clothes and always bright colors. And that wonderful wide-brimmed straw hat with the rainbow ribbons stretching down her back! Her father once said that Mrs. Davis had been the best cheerleader in the entire high school, and Madeline could see why.

She was glad the village was nearly deserted. She needed time to prepare herself for her summer friends. She wanted to wait for Charles to come. Charles had written that they would be arriving earlier than usual this summer. Charles would get things going and rally their friends around. He was a doer, and Madeline always needed a nudge. She depended on Charles. He would take care of her this summer. Most of the village people her age were too cliquey, with their little private jokes. They lived in the village year round, had gone to school together and attended parties together and sailed together, forever it seemed. Madeline was grateful for her two cousins! They were "summer people"—just like she was.

From the very beginning, even though he was two years older than she, Madeline and Charles had always been close friends. Lisa was Madeline's age exactly, but she had always been left behind dressing her dolls while Charles and Madeline and Flash went exploring. Now Lisa was always the last one to get her sailboat rigged, because she spent so much time dressing herself and putting on eye make-up. Charles thought his sister was a pain.

"Paris was Lisa's ruination," Charles maintained. And he and Madeline had had to laugh when Lisa's boat capsized last year, and she rose from the water with black streaks running down her face and her eyelashes pasted together.

As Madeline opened the car door, she suddenly saw Arthur Whittington emerge from the hardware store. Arthur was a good friend of Charles's—a tall, handsome, old man for his age. He had an insatiable curiosity about mathematics, an intense dislike of English or any other language, and only a slight tolerance for history. Unfortunately, he also had a younger brother named Henry, who was the outstanding scholar of the seventh grade. Mrs. Whittington often said that she would like to put them both in a popcorn bowl and shake it so hard that the two of them got their parts all mixed up.

Arthur had been secretary and treasurer of the secret club, because he was so organized, and they had many records to keep: of their weekly dues which covered the cost of candy and sodas, and of their pay from the drugstore, the hardware store and the grocery. He also scheduled their weekly work assignments. Madeline had always admired Arthur's orderly, mechanical mind. So had her father, who had often asked Arthur for help on his boats, and Arthur had joined them for summer sails.

Now, he appeared, carrying a paint can in one hand and an anchor in the other. Around his neck was a neatly coiled rope. Madeline would have recognized him simply by the objects surrounding him. She didn't need to see the perfectly combed red hair or the tailored button-down shirt.

In panic, she ducked into the car and slid down in the front seat. Flash started barking, and she knew Arthur had probably seen the license plate and was on his way over to the car right this very minute. She felt hot and nervous as she slid farther down onto the floor.

Then Madeline heard her mother greet him. Her mother, too, had always liked Arthur. All mothers and fathers liked Arthur. He was what all parents call clean-cut. Why, one Sunday last summer he even wore a suit and vest to church. Charles used to say in exasperation that he was the universal example of the perfect teenage boy.

"That boy will amount to something," her father had always said, when Arthur had helped him tune up the engine on a boat.

"He's so polite," her mother had always said. "His parents must be proud of him."

"Yuck!" Madeline thought. Still, she had to admit, Arthur was nicer than most of the others. And Charles said Arthur had a great sense of humor.

But Madeline didn't want to see Arthur today, not this minute, not like this. She felt flushed and shaky. She needed Charles around.

Why was her mother always so friendly? Why did she have to speak to everybody? Why did she have to draw attention to them? Madeline felt so embarrassed.

"Oh, thank you, Arthur," her mother was saying. "If you could just put the packages way in the back, that would be fine."

Madeline sighed in relief. Her mother must have seen her lying there on the floor.

She heard the bags clunk down and the tailgate slam shut.

More relief.

"Thank you so much, Arthur. Hope we'll see you soon. Charles comes next week."

Oh, come on, Mom, Madeline thought. The agony of it all. She buried her head in her knees until she felt very small.

"See you before then. Yes, indeed," Arthur said. And as he walked by the car door, he added, "Bye, Madeline."

Madeline was mortified. She wanted to scream and dissolve completely, immediately.

"I could pass out," she uttered weakly, as her mother climbed in behind the wheel.

"Maybe he thought you had," her mother whispered, smiling.

Madeline regained her composure as her mother backed the car away from the grocery store. Flash nuzzled her hair.

"Why do I act like that, Flash?" she asked. It was easier to ask Flash than to question her mother. Flash presented no discussion. Anyway, she already knew the answer. She wasn't good with boys. She never knew how to act around them, the way Lisa did. Madeline always giggled too much or laughed too loudly or shook her head too hard or stumbled when she really meant to lean. The only safe place for her to be with a boy was in a boat, with the wind blowing so hard that she couldn't open her mouth.

They drove in silence down the main street, past the post office, the library, and the two churches. Madeline noticed that the new addition to the library was exactly suited to the sand-colored gothic style of the old part. The library had always looked distinctive in the village. It was the only non-white structure around, and oddly enough, not an old New England style. Her mother always said it reminded her of California. The enormous rhododendron bush on the corner was in full, luscious bloom, and it looked as if it were on fire. Madeline noticed that the Episcopal church needed painting again. It needed painting every year. That was the trouble with stark colonial white. The clock in the steeple of the Congregational church chimed the hour of five as they rounded the corner past the old Simpson house.

The huge Victorian house used to be an inn and

had balconies and mysterious little towers jutting out all over it. Madeline used to fancy herself perched on the highest balcony on the very top of the house, surrounded by adoring admirers, laughing softly and leaning gracefully against the railing. But her father had told her that the balcony was really a sad place. It was called a widow's walk because in the old days ladies stood there watching and waiting for their husbands to come home from the sea. Often the husbands never came, and the ladies always cried. Now, Madeline could see that it too needed a coat of paint. All the curlicues were chipping, and the porches looked gray. It must have been a bad winter.

However, the roses along Mrs. Chapman's fence didn't seem to have minded the cold and the snow. They were thicker and more beautiful than ever. Mrs. Chapman never really liked yellow roses much, but they liked her, and they were loyal to the fence year after year after year. Mrs. Chapman and Madeline often laughed about that.

"Mom," Madeline finally said, as they drew nearer the summer house, "could we go by the beach—I mean, go the long way home?"

"Of course, Mad, if you want to. We have plenty of time. Aunt Ede won't be home from the newspaper until six." Her mother turned the car down one of the side streets. "Do you want to stop at the beach by the water?"

"Okay," Madeline answered.

The village beach was at the edge of town, not far from the summer house. It was a strip of sand about three blocks long, interrupted by one lonely lifeguard chair, high on stilts, looking out over mushy sandbars at low tide.

Her mother pulled up against the guard rail and stopped the car. "The low-tide smell," she remarked, "I'll never get used to it." Her mother had spent her summers on a lake in northern California, and lakes don't have tide smells.

"You never smell it out there," Madeline nodded, and she gazed far out to where the waves began. A strange homesickness took hold of her.

The few people left on the beach were pulling up umbrellas and folding up chairs and starting for home. The early June days were never as warm as they seemed.

"Mom, I've wondered about something for a long time. Could I ask you something?" Madeline felt odd talking to her mother like that, but there was no one else around. There was something she just had to know now, and she couldn't wait for Aunt Ede. "Mom, do you believe all those things that Dad used to say?"

"What things?" her mother asked gently.

"Those things about when he died, about what would happen to him?"

"Your father believed them."

"Well, yes, Mom, I know *he* believed them. But do you?"

"I believe that your father didn't just die and that was the end of it. I believe that life goes on, just as before, but somewhere else."

"That's what I mean, Mom."

"Yes, I guess I believe what your father always said. Yes, I do," her mother decided.

"Well, where do you think his spirit is? Do you think it's in the house, waiting for us? How will he watch over us? How will he still love us—like he said?" Madeline's voice had grown tight, and tears burned her eyes. "I just don't see how he can do all those things that he promised."

Her mother turned to her and put a reassuring hand on Madeline's arm. "I'm sure he will find a way. And I'm sure he will be with us in a very special way, and the house will be even more special to us."

Madeline turned to her mother and tried to smile. "I guess maybe it *is* nice to be back," she said as they drove toward home. She felt calmer and the memories of last summer seemed less overwhelming.

It was only when they passed through the gate and she saw the house again that she felt the ache return.

MEMORIES
IN THE HOUSE

THE stone wall that ran parallel to the road was typical of Connecticut. Random rocks, piled one on top of another in no definite pattern, finally settled down over the years into a solid and enduring fence. Aunt Ede said her stone wall was there before the soldiers came and probably helped to hide the house. When the summer house had been built, Madeline's father had extended the wall so the summer house would be safe too. Adequate protection from the road, Madeline thought, but last summer the harm had come from the water side.

"Aunt Ede's car isn't around," Madeline's mother said, as she drove into the garage. "Let's go inside and start unpacking. Aunt Ede said she'd have supper for us around eight."

"Okay." Madeline got out of the car slowly. She

opened the back door for Flash, who was pawing the window in excitement. Flash stumbled down and disappeared around the corner. Madeline walked from the garage hesitantly and stood looking at the house. It needs painting too, she thought.

The sparkling white of last summer had dulled considerably, and ugly brown rust marks streaked from the shutter pins. Madeline's father would never have put up with that, not for a minute. The painters would start immediately, and, in a couple of weeks, after insistent coaxing, the job would be done. Also, several bricks on the chimney had come loose and were crumbling away. That should be repaired. She and her mother had plenty of work to do. She felt uneasy, standing there in the driveway, with the house, in that condition, looking at her.

"Coming, Mad?" her mother broke in, reaching above the doorsill. "The key should be up here some place."

"I'll be along in a minute." Madeline walked around to the side of the house, so she could see the water. "Look over here, Mom. Mr. Robinson must have planted the vegetable garden." She knew Aunt Ede couldn't have done it. When Uncle Harold died and Aunt Ede took over the newspaper, there wasn't time any more for a vegetable garden. "That really was nice of Mr. Robinson," she said.

Mr. Robinson had dug it up and planted it in neat rows, just as her father had always done, with labels and stakes at either end. She walked around, reading: "Peas, carrots, tomatoes, and bush beans." Bush beans were her father's favorite. They were punctual and productive and seemed to try harder than the rest, traits for which her father had admired them. Madeline had loved to help her father in the garden, pulling up weeds and thinning the plants, but she wasn't so sure about tending the garden without him.

"That was wonderful of Mr. Robinson to go to all that trouble," her mother said, as she came up beside Madeline. "Makes you appreciate a small village like this." Her mother turned and went back to the house.

Madeline walked slowly around to the front yard. She was in no hurry to go inside. Flash was standing on the grass, his front paws on the seawall, staring toward the beach. Suddenly, Madeline felt a sharp pain in her stomach and her legs went spongy. She couldn't bring herself to look at the beach. He might be there still, lying as if he were planning to sun himself beneath the moon. Her throat went dry. She could feel the hurt again when she had screamed for her mother and the sound of her mother's sandals as they had clicked over the wall. He was so cold, and her tears were so hot, and Flash had tried so hard to wake him! Then they came and took him away. But she had run down the sand, to the farthest end of the beach, and she never saw him go.

Flash was making those same sounds now, quiet

sounds, but urgent. Madeline finally braced herself and followed his eyes. There were five swans marching back and forth, completely oblivious to the enemy watching them. She felt relieved.

"Too bad, Flash. I will *not* help you over to chase birds. Come on with me," she commanded. Flash looked disappointed, but he dutifully turned and followed Madeline, with a drooping tail.

"The house looks like a flower shop! It's just beautiful!" Madeline's mother exclaimed, opening the front door.

"Oh," sighed Madeline. The scent of lilacs and honeysuckle was stifling. There were bouquets of flowers in every corner of the living room. Madeline was taken aback. It looked to her like a funeral parlor. But, she didn't say so. "Really something," she stammered. "Mr. Robinson?"

"Maybe Aunt Ede. What a thoughtful thing to do!"

Madeline didn't agree. Aunt Ede would never have done a thing like that. She felt dizzy. Why couldn't people just leave them alone? That was the trouble with a small town like this! Everybody meddling, trying to be nice. It was bad enough to actually be inside the house again, without repeating the atmosphere of last summer. The day after her father had died, there were flowers all over the place, and now here they were again, choking the room. "It's a bad joke," she whispered, and she ran upstairs before her mother could see her reaction.

At the top of the stairs, she opened the window to let in some fresh air, but the acrid odor of low tide was still around, the smell of snails and crabs and clams and oysters eating one another, the smell of death. She couldn't decide which was worse, the smell of the flowers or the smell of the beach.

"Madeline," her mother called. "Where are you?"

"Up here, Mom." She heard the bell buoy at the mouth of the harbor. Its clang was a deep moan. She quickly closed the window. In another hour, the tide would roll back in with a pure, clean smell. She would open all the windows then and take a deep breath.

As she started down the stairs, a car appeared in the driveway, honking.

"Aunt Ede's here," her mother called. Madeline swung out the door and into Aunt Ede's arms.

"Welcome home, princess!" Aunt Ede hugged her. Madeline could feel how lanky she was and trim for a woman of sixty. Aunt Ede would never have to worry about a middle-aged spread. "Drop everything, Carol, and come over to the house now," she said to Madeline's mother. "You have all summer long to unpack."

Madeline walked across the yard ahead of them.

"It doesn't seem possible it's just been two months since I saw you last." Aunt Ede had an arm

around her mother as they walked along. "How did the show turn out?"

"Not bad," her mother answered. "I sold three paintings, and the gallery commissioned three more for the fall exhibit."

Aunt Ede beamed. "That is *terrific!* Wouldn't Sam be proud of you!"

"I guess he would," she heard her mother say.

Is, Madeline silently corrected.

"How's the paper?"

"Great! But," Aunt Ede wailed, "we need some news badly. We need something to *happen* around here beside who's talking at the next PTA meeting and who's buying whose house. The ice storm and the blizzard took care of two weeks. One whole issue for each—fantastic coverage—" she laughed— "but not much since then. How about it?" she called to Madeline. "How about making some sailing news this summer?" Her voice trailed off as they reached the front steps.

"Come on, Flash!" Madeline called.

"We'll wait for you," Aunt Ede chimed as she opened the door. "We should all slow down like Flash and enjoy ourselves," she patted him. Flash licked her hand in greeting.

Madeline hesitated before following Aunt Ede into the kitchen. She glanced at her mother, who also had stopped for a moment before entering the house. It was as if the memories in Aunt Ede's house were even more potent for her mother than the memories in the summer house. This was the house that her father had known and had loved for a lifetime. Suddenly, Madeline's mother held out her hand and, with Flash behind them, they went in together.

As Aunt Ede and her mother began gathering things for supper, Madeline looked all around the well-remembered room.

Grandmother Anderson had restored the house when Aunt Ede and Madeline's father had been little children. Aunt Ede loved to tell the story of the old coal stove and the day it was removed from the center of the kitchen.

"There was this big hole in the ceiling, where the stovepipes had been, that looked right up to heaven," Aunt Ede said. And she and her brother had begged Grandfather Anderson not to cover it up.

"Let's put a window there," Madeline's father had suggested.

And that's exactly what Grandfather Anderson had done. "Wouldn't be right to shut out heaven," he had agreed. To this day, heaven had indeed blessed all of Aunt Ede's plants that hung beneath the skylight.

The old butcher-block table in the corner always held a rough wooden bowl filled with fresh fruit. Over the table Grandmother Anderson's prize lamp hung from the ceiling. It had been her favorite wedding present—a frosted-glass shade with a painted scene of snow-laden Vermont. There was a little house in the distance and pine trees beside a road half-hidden by snow. The scene always made Madeline feel cool, even on a hot summer's night, when Aunt Ede turned the lamp on at dusk.

"It's better than air conditioning," Aunt Ede would say. "Just look at it hard, make a wish, and hop right onto that road. Really can give you a chill, if you try." Madeline felt it once just like that. It was fun to hop in and out of pictures sometimes.

Flash brushed by her on his way to the stove, his nose sniffing the air. "We won't forget you," Aunt Ede laughed. "We'll fix you a feast."

"He's glad to be back," Madeline said, smiling. Then she added eagerly, "When are Charles and Lisa arriving?"

"The end of next week. Charles won't have too long before he goes out West."

Madeline's voice dropped. "Out West. Where?"

"Didn't he write you? He's going to stay with his uncle in Oregon most of the summer."

"You mean, be a lumberjack?" her mother broke in. "How wonderful for him!"

Madeline stood still, staring at Aunt Ede in disbelief.

"Harvey got him a summer job on the river up there," Aunt Ede's voice droned on.

Madeline's mother caught the disappointment, a sense of abandonment, on Madeline's face. "Lisa will be around though, won't she, Edith?"

"Oh, yes. Lisa will be sailing."

"Yuck," Madeline mumbled as her eyes started to fill. It's not fair. Charles shouldn't be going away this summer. Not this summer when she's all alone.

"He'll be around long enough to get things going," Aunt Ede assured them. "Charles is just like his father—an organizer. He'll have the sailing lessons going even before they start."

"You know, Carol, it's funny how my boys turned out." She was setting the table. "When Harold died, Michael was the one who took over the thinking job around here—even though he was only five. He made all the lists and counted the pennies. And Harvey was the one who carried the toys around for his brother and moved the chairs out of the way, and he was only three. Harvey liked the muscle work. Now today, they're still like that—all grown up and working—just the way they used to be, in the same sort of job."

"What was Sam like?" Madeline's mother asked, having been caught up in Aunt Ede's reminiscing.

"Sam was everything," Aunt Ede said genuinely. "He was a thinker and a doer, with a soaring imagination. Well," she laughed, motioning to the skylight "he never wanted to shut out heaven, and he never did."

Madeline had sat down at the table and was fingering one of the apples.

"I always said," Aunt Ede went on, as she fixed the supper, "you were the best thing that ever happened to Sam. I had just about given up on him. He brought all those women around but nothing came of it. A man gets to be over forty and never gets married. It seemed hopeless. Then, when he called me from California and told me about you, I could have run it on page one." Madeline's mother had sat down and helped herself to some grapes. She always liked to hear Aunt Ede talk about their romance. "You know, Carol, to tell you the truth, I would have welcomed you even if you had had two heads. I was so happy he had found someone to love." She clapped her hands. "And then to see you—so much younger and so beautiful—and so much in love with *him*—well!"

Madeline felt a little uncomfortable, as if she might be trespassing on hallowed ground before her time, but she loved to hear stories about her father.

"What was the book he was out there promoting?" Aunt Ede asked again, as she poured the ice tea.

Madeline's mother knew Aunt Ede knew, but they always played out the same conversation, and they both enjoyed it.

"It was the one on Italy," her mother answered.

"That's right. Then he up and takes you there on your honeymoon to show you all the ruins."

"I got a better interview." Her mother laughed. "At least I saw everything firsthand."

"And you didn't have to sail around the world in his forty-foot yawl."

"Ugh," her mother shuddered. She always got seasick just looking at a boat.

"Sam was doubly blessed. He had Madeline to sail with," Aunt Ede nodded. "How about some supper?"

When the dishes were finished and the kitchen cleaned up, Madeline took Flash for a walk in the yard. Purposely avoiding the beach, she and Flash ended up sitting under the large maple tree between the two houses.

"It won't be much fun with Charles away," Madeline told Flash.

Flash wagged his tail in agreement.

"And dumb Lisa will spend all summer combing her hair and fixing up her eyes and saying all those silly French words to all the boys. You know, Flash, I bet she's even bigger around the top *this* summer."

Flash wagged his tail again.

"And with Charles gone and Dad gone—" Her eyes smarted and she blinked. "Mom said it would be all right this summer, but that was before she knew about Charles."

Flash crawled closer to her and lay his head in her lap. "Well, I have you," she stated, pulling herself together. "And you won't leave me, I know." She leaned down and kissed his ear.

"Goodnight, Edith," her mother called, as she came toward Madeline. "Ready, Mad? We've got a big day tomorrow."

"Goodnight, Aunt Ede. Thank you for supper."

The house felt chilly as Madeline started upstairs to bed.

"Call Flash upstairs with you, Mad."

Madeline stopped at the head of the stairs. "Come here, Flash. Come on, boy."

Flash ascended the stairs with effort. Madeline watched him, reaching over to help him up the last few steps. She wished now that Flash were a small dog. She would have liked to pick him up and carry him in her arms.

"Good boy!" she praised him. "Let's go to my room."

Madeline's room was in the front of the house, over the kitchen wing. It was easy for her to slip down the back stairs for late-night snacks. Many times her father had joined her.

"How does this sound?" he had said, reading her part of his latest chapter.

"Great!" she always answered, because it always was.

Madeline typed for him, and she listened to him. Sometimes, she researched for him, too, especially during the last few years.

"She takes better notes than I do," her father had stated. "Her majesty will be the literary queen!"

But Madeline assured him that when she grew up, she was going to be a veterinarian—that is, after she had sailed around the world!

"I'll make sure that Flash lives forever, that he never grows old."

"He may grow old," her father suggested, "but he *will* live forever!"

She really had doubted her father's theory about living forever until now, back at the summer house.

Wearily she sank down on the floor by her bed. The sharp pain she had hoped was gone forever came back, weakening her legs and pushing into her throat until she could hardly recognize her own voice. "He's here," she said aloud. "I know he's here."

Flash whimpered and pressed close to her, anxiously pawing her jeans. Madeline hugged him as tightly as she could, burying her face in his soft fur. Tears welled in her eyes. "I just wish I could see him," she whispered, "just once more."

The next morning Madeline was up early. She had had trouble sleeping, and it seemed useless to stay in bed any longer. She started unpacking her duffle bag stuffed full with T-shirts and shorts and blue jeans. The one dress that was left over from last summer still hung out of the way in the corner of her closet. It was merely a token gesture to her mother that she included it in her worldly possessions.

A short time later she was finished unpacking, had made her bed, was dressed and downstairs, eating her breakfast. The flowers in the living room had begun to wilt a little. She was thankful for that.

"Hi, Madeline!"

She recognized the voice at the screen door. "Hi, Arthur." She felt flushed. "What do you want?" That sounded rude, so she added quickly, "Come on in." Again she had said the wrong thing. What would she do with him now? What would she say to him? As Arthur walked into the kitchen she suddenly wanted Charles or her mother or anyone. "Uh, would you like some orange juice?"

"Sure."

Madeline poured him a glass, standing with her back to him so he couldn't see her hand shaking. "Charles comes next week, but he won't be here long."

"I know. He wrote me about it."

Madeline was annoyed. Charles hadn't written her.

"I wouldn't mind doing that myself, if you could roll logs from a boat," Arthur said. "How about going out on a boat this morning? It's a good day."

"My boat's not ready," Madeline answered nervously. "I mean—I haven't been down to the Yacht Club yet to check on *Banana Peel*."

"That's okay," Arthur said. "I have a boat ready." He smiled. "That is, if you can stand a motor boat."

"Well. . ." Madeline began. Then she heard her mother on the stairs. Oh, thank heaven, she wouldn't be left alone with him any longer. Her confidence grew with her mother's approaching steps. "I'd like to another time. I really would, but today I have to help mother." She finished the sentence just in time. She knew her mother would have insisted that she go.

"Good morning, Arthur," her mother said, sounding pleased. "Will you stay for breakfast?"

"Oh, thank you very much, but I'm on my way now." He bowed to her mother. "Sorry you can't join me, Madeline."

"But, Madeline would—"

"See you later, Arthur. Thanks!"

"Madeline," her mother's voice was stern. "Did Arthur want you to go sailing?"

"Yes, Mom. But I can't today. I just can't."

"Madeline, why? It's a beautiful day."

"I don't know Arthur that well." She stumbled over the words. "I mean, he's Charles's friend."

Her mother said slowly, "Sounds as if he'd like to be your friend, too."

"He's just trying to be nice." Madeline knew she sounded defensive.

"Well, what's wrong with that?" Her mother sounded impatient.

"Because he feels sorry for me."

"*Why?*" her mother asked, definitely impatient now.

"Because of Dad. Because Dad died like that. He doesn't really want to be friends. He just feels bad for me." Madeline rushed on, "All the kids around here feel that way. I just *know* they do. They don't *really* like people like us. They never have."

Madeline's mother poured herself some coffee. "Like us?"

"People who just come out here for the summer. They call us transients. Charles knows."

There was a noise in the driveway. Madeline looked out the window and quickly headed for the back stairs. "Tell them I'm not up yet," she whispered to her mother. "*Please,* Mom!"

Tory and Lee descended from their bicycles and walked toward the back door. Tory was giggling as usual. Lee followed her, smiling.

Madeline's mother opened the door. "Good morning, girls. How nice to see you."

Madeline peeked out her bedroom window from behind the curtains.

"Madeline's not downstairs now," her mother said, apologetically.

"Would you please tell her we were by, Mrs. Anderson?"

Both the girls looked really good, Madeline thought, peering further around the curtains. Tory had cut her hair, and it hugged her face in curly puffs. It made her look older, Madeline thought. She probably wears a bra now, too.

"Tell Madeline the Yacht Club has been redone, and we've got some really neat new plans for this summer!"

"Really great," Lee aped eagerly.

"I'll tell Madeline. I know she'll be anxious to see you."

"Thank you very much, Mrs. Anderson," Tory said. "Tell her we'll wait for her at the Yacht Club!" She skipped over to her bicycle.

"Thanks a lot," repeated Lee. "It's awfully nice seeing you back!"

"Why wouldn't we be back?" Madeline muttered to herself. "It's just like I thought. They're still thinking about Dad and feeling sorry for me."

Madeline's mother waved to them as they climbed on their bicycles and rode off, just as Aunt Ede came across the driveway.

After a few minutes, Madeline slowly made her way downstairs, dreading what her mother would say. Halfway down, she heard her mother talking. "Edith, what should I do about Madeline? She doesn't want to see any of her friends. They all want to see her. She's had visitors all morning."

"She probably feels awkward. Things are different this year. Sam's gone. She can't face happiness—at least, not so much of it—just yet. I guess she just doesn't want them to say they're sorry." Aunt Ede hugged her mother's shoulders as Madeline walked into the kitchen. "Give her time," she whispered.

"Oh, Madeline." Her mother looked up as Madeline self-consciously slid into a chair.

"You know what I think I'll do now," her mother decided. "I'll call the painters about the house, and then I'll do some painting myself." She left the kitchen, saying over her shoulder, "Tory and Lee were by, Mad. They're down at the club."

Madeline got up and walked over to Aunt Ede. "Thank you, Aunt Ede," she said, kissing her aunt's cheek. "I heard what you told Mom. And I will be okay after a while. After Charles comes."

"I know you will, princess." She stood. "Well, I'm off to work." She looked around. "Where's Flash?"

"Oh, he's still upstairs. I haven't brought him down yet. I have to help him now, up and down."

"Well, he needs his sunshine. You'd better go get him. See you tonight!"

Madeline and Flash joined her mother on the front lawn. A flock of swans was floating just beyond Aunt Ede's dock.

"Are you going to paint the swans?" Madeline asked.

"Maybe," her mother answered. "Have you ever seen one up close?"

Madeline shook her head. "You always told me to keep my distance." She followed her mother's eyes as she stared off into space. "Why?"

"Their eyes are masked. You know what I mean, Mad, like the half-masks that children wear on Halloween or the masks that elegant ladies carried to fancy balls a long time ago—harlequin masks. Then, when the ladies wanted to hide who they were, they held the masks up to their eyes. Funny, how swans have eyes like that, hidden and mysterious," her mother mused. "You don't realize it until you see one up close."

"I guess I did see one up close once—a long time ago—yes, I did. I don't think that one wore a mask. I don't remember it, anyway." But, she did remember that swan, the very big one, the one that followed *The Great Lady* that day last summer.

The week passed quickly. The summer house received its first coat of fresh paint, and Madeline and her mother planted the flower garden beside the garage. She had never before helped her mother in a garden, and she discovered, much to her amazement, that her mother was a lot fussier than her father had been. Her mother took the whole thing quite seriously, and they didn't talk at all.

Madeline had never realized before just how much work her father did around the house. She took it for granted that the grass would grow and the flowers bloom, that it all happened automatically. Up to now, she thought the only things that ever needed care were the boat and the vegetables.

The day before Charles and Lisa were to arrive, her mother decided to tackle her father's study. Madeline had dreaded the thought. She definitely did not want to disturb that room. She almost wished that Arthur would take her sailing or that the others would come and force her out to the pizza place.

"We'll fix up the room so you can entertain your friends," her mother suggested enthusiastically.

Madeline winced. In that room—never. But maybe she would ask them over sometime. That is, if her mother didn't suggest it again.

They packed up all her father's books and put them into boxes to give to the library. Then her mother took up to her room all his personal things, except for the figurehead from his first boat which Madeline wanted. Someday she would put it back where it belonged, on the front of a proud ship. She was exhausted when she finally went to bed. And she couldn't wait until tomorrow, when Charles would come and everything would be all right again.

That night, the channel buoys clanged repeatedly, making a terrible racket. Madeline never remembered hearing them sounding so loud before.

And the waves were pounding incessantly against the seawall with increasing force. It sounded as if a terrible storm were coming up. But when she finally got out of bed to look out the window, the sky was filled with stars.

Down in the kitchen, she heated some milk to help her sleep. She was so tired, and she felt strangely uneasy. There were cold drafts rushing around her, and she began to shiver. Memories seemed to hover in the shadows of the room and fill every corner. Suddenly she sat down at the table and began to cry.

Flash struggled to his feet from his pillow at the bottom of the stairs and walked over to put his head in Madeline's lap.

"Do you think he's here, Flash?" Madeline cried softly. "Do you think he's watching us?" She raised her voice. "Do you think he's mad about the room? I mean about how Mom changed his room." Her head shook back and forth. "Mom shouldn't have changed his room. I didn't want to change it. It was Mom's idea." Her voice grew shrill, as the tears streamed down her face and the words stung her throat.

The next moment, her mother appeared at her side. Madeline jumped away from her, out of the chair. Flash fell backwards.

"The room, Mom. You shouldn't have changed Dad's room." She was shaking all over, and her hair fell in damp strings down her face. "Oh, Mom, why did he leave us? Why did he die?"

Madeline's mother put her arms around her. She said nothing. Slowly Madeline began to relax, and she finally dropped her head on her mother's shoulder.

"It will be all right, Madeline, I promise you."

Madeline slumped back again into the chair, her head in her arms on the table.

"Do you want to talk a minute?" her mother asked.

"Okay." Madeline didn't look up.

Her mother sat down in the chair beside her. "If you'd go out with your friends and get away from the house, you'd feel much better. Tory and Lee have come by here at least six times this past week, and you say you're always busy. And Arthur has been running a steady course in his boat back and forth in front of the house. Go out with them. Have fun the way you always used to."

"I can't yet, Mom, I just can't. I can't pretend I'm happy, because I'm not."

"Even when Charles comes tomorrow?"

"That's just it, Mom. Charles will come, and then he'll go again, almost right away." She started to cry softly. "Aunt Ede said that Harvey called, and he wants Charles out there right after the Fourth of July. He'll hardly be here at all this summer."

"But Lisa will be here, and all the others."

Madeline suddenly stopped crying and looked up. "I can't stay, Mom. I can't stay here this summer. I know you said it would be all right, but it isn't." Her voice suddenly was steady and reasonable. "I can't stay here and watch them all being so happy and watch them all trying so hard to make me feel happy and all the time I'll know what they're thinking—how sorry they all feel for me!"

"They don't feel sorry for you, Madeline. *You* feel sorry for you!" Her mother's voice grew cool. "You feel sorry for yourself—nobody else does." She pulled her chair over close to Madeline. "Look, Madeline, you have stayed around this house for a week. You have planted the garden. You have cleaned up the yard. You have rearranged the house. You have painted Aunt Ede's dock." Her mother ticked off the list precisely. "Madeline, there is nothing more for you to do." She spoke very calmly. Madeline sat still, looking at her. "Tomorrow, we are going to find a boat to keep at the dock. A boat for you and Flash and all your friends. A boat with a small cabin—not *The Great Lady*—but a good lady."

Madeline bristled. "*No!* I don't want a boat. I don't want a boat ever again at that dock!" Her voice rose, and she started to tremble, as she pulled herself out of her chair. "Tomorrow I am going back to the city! I've made up my mind! I'm getting out of here! I've been thinking about it, and that's the only thing I can do!"

Her mother spoke sharply. "And cop out!" She looked Madeline straight in the eyes. "You can sure do that!" Madeline stared back at her mother, hearing her continue in clipped, punctuated words: "Madeline, you are not a baby any more. Face it! You must change! You have mourned for your father long enough!"

Her mother stood before her—so young, so beautiful, and so in control. Madeline's eyes grew fierce, and she set her jaw. "Who are you to tell me what's enough!" Her words stabbed the air. "For that matter, who are *you* to tell *me* anything?" Her mother stood up quickly and reached out her hand to Madeline. "You keep away from me! You don't tell me what to do!" She backed off, and her face was colored with rage. "I don't have to change! My father loved me just the way I am." She began to sob. "He tells me what to do." She started walking toward the back stairs. "And if *he* wants me to stay here this summer, I'll stay."

She turned and ran up the stairs to her room closing the door and pressing hard against it with her aching body. She felt that her anger and grief would blow her into tiny pieces around the room.

Slowly she made her way to bed, clenching her fists and forcing her legs forward. She heard her mother's footsteps come up the stairs and stop in front of her door. Madeline held her breath until her mother moved away on down the hall. Then she let her shoulders sag with relief. Downstairs, she could hear Flash moving restlessly around the kitchen. Her face was wet and sticky with tears, and she hurt all over, but the lump in her throat felt smaller now, and the house at last became silent, calm and still.

ARTHUR

"AUNT Ede, I'm all finished, and I've cleaned up the kitchen," Madeline called up the front stairs. "When are we going?"

"Right away! I'll be right down!"

Madeline stopped by the mirror in the dining room and combed her hair. "Wait on the porch, Flash, and we'll be right back with Charles and Lisa! Then we'll have some fun!"

"You're up awfully early for a Saturday morning," Aunt Ede commented as they climbed in the car.

"I thought everybody in the country rose with the sun," Madeline replied with a laugh. "Besides, Charles and Lisa come today!"

"In exactly twelve minutes," Aunt Ede said, as

she waited at the only traffic light in the village.
"Why the baking spree in my kitchen?"

"Well, I had to welcome them home with
something special. It's a giant French-flag cookie!"
Madeline said proudly.

"Bien entendu!" Aunt Ede laughed. "Where's your
mother this morning? She's usually up early."

"I guess she's tired." Madeline hoped her guilt
didn't show. She was suddenly nervous. "You know
how much Mom was doing for the last few weeks
before we came. She's been awfully busy, running
around." The words spilled out. "She finally went
to that TV station about getting a job. Like the one
she had in California a long time ago, that
educational thing."

"No kidding! I think that's great! What did they
say?"

"I guess it looks pretty good. After the first of the
year, they thought. Mom said that painting pictures
just wasn't enough, and it's too lonely."

"Of course it is," Aunt Ede agreed. "Your mother
is young. She deserves a life." Madeline stiffened
slightly. "Don't you think so?"

"Yes, I guess."

They pulled into the commuter parking lot at the
railroad station. Everyone going to or from the
village passed through that place.

"Well, there they are!" Aunt Ede pointed to the
airport limousine.

"Yuck," Madeline whispered as she and Aunt Ede

walked over to the curb where several people were struggling with luggage. Madeline recognized Lisa right away. The only one not struggling with luggage, Lisa was talking animatedly to four great-looking boys who were hovering over her, only too pleased and honored to do her struggling for her.

Aunt Ede caught Lisa's eye. *"Pardonnez moi."* Lisa turned to her admirers.

"Good grief," Madeline said aloud.

"Right!" a deep voice agreed.

Madeline turned to face Charles. She hugged him tight. "Oh, Charles, I'm so glad to see you!" she whispered. "Lisa's the same as ever, I see."

"Worse," Charles noted. "She took the continent by storm, as they say." Both he and Madeline chuckled.

"Who are the boys?"

"Exchange students on their way to some summer camp up north." He sighed. "It was quite a trip!"

Lisa waltzed over, grabbing Aunt Ede and Madeline together. *"Bonjour! Comment ça va?"* One side of her golden hair was caught provocatively behind an ear, while the other side cascaded to her waist. That hair style will never do on a boat, Madeline thought. She'll get it caught in a halyard and hang herself from the mast. Madeline relished the image.

"I brought you something, Madeline," Lisa said, reaching into her purse. She took out a photograph of Madeline and her father standing on the foredeck of *The Great Lady*, taken right before they had set sail that last afternoon. Flash sat at attention by Madeline's side. Lisa had put the picture in a silver frame with tiny gold flowers etched around the border. Madeline glanced at it quickly and tried to smile, but the corners of her mouth started to tremble, and all too suddenly her eyes smarted and started to fill. Lisa didn't seem to notice.

"Thank you, Lisa," she said softly.

"How's everybody?" Charles asked, as he loaded suitcases into the trunk.

"I haven't really seen anyone," Madeline said. "I've been helping get the house all fixed up." She avoided mentioning her mother. "Arthur's the only one I've really talked to—and not for long."

Charles and Lisa climbed into the back seat, while Madeline slid into the car beside Aunt Ede. She opened the glove compartment and put Lisa's present carefully away in the very back. She couldn't bear to look at it again. "Charles, I didn't know you were going away this summer."

"Didn't know for sure myself until just a while ago. Seems like too good a trip to pass up."

"I wish you weren't going," Madeline said, and her voice was sad.

Charles leaned forward and put his hand on her shoulder. "Don't fret, little cousin, I'm leaving you in good hands—Arthur's."

Arthur's good hands fixed engines and designed motors and kept books.

"Who's going to crew for me?" Madeline asked, a little irked at Charles's presumptuous handling of her summer. "Arthur never sails. He just fusses around the motorboats."

"Tory will crew for you, the way she always has."

"I mean every day in class. Tory's never down there every day. She has tennis lessons and swim practice and riding."

"So, Arthur will be your fun everyday crew."

"Arthur, fun?" Madeline stopped abruptly. Charles and Lisa were here at last and Charles's time was short. And here she was already arguing and being unpleasant. It was just that Charles was being selfish about his own plans, leaving her floundering about the Sound with Arthur Whittington and a whole bunch of mechanical terms and dubious reactions.

A chilly silence filled the car.

Finally Lisa spoke, changing the subject. "Where's Carol?" she asked Aunt Ede. Lisa had long since asked Madeline's mother whether to call her Aunt Carol. And Madeline's mother had said, "Please don't. It would make me feel too old!"

"Madeline says she's resting up," Aunt Ede answered. "She's about to become a working girl again."

"Très bien!" Lisa exclaimed, as they drove through the gate and approached the house.

A short while later, when Madeline's mother came

in by Aunt Ede's kitchen door, Madeline went out by the front door in search of Charles. She couldn't face her mother quite yet.

Charles was down on the dock, talking to Arthur. He sure doesn't waste any time pawning me off, Madeline thought indignantly.

"Hi, Madeline!" Arthur called.

"Hey, come on down!" Charles joined in. Madeline hated how nice they were trying to be. It was so phony. She turned around quickly and ran as fast as she could to the summer house. Flash met her on the porch. She pulled him inside and huddled down on the floor next to him, hugging him tight.

"I'm such a mess," she whispered over and over, as tears trickled down her cheeks. "Mother hates me! Charles hates me! Arthur hates me! What's wrong with me?" Flash licked her face. "You're the only one who likes me."

"Madeline what's the matter? What's wrong?" Charles was at the door.

Madeline slouched farther into the corner. I'm such a fool, she thought. When Charles opened the door, she slipped out to the kitchen.

"Hey, Madeline!" he shouted. She pulled herself together and stood very straight, combing her hair.

"Out here!" she called.

"What's the matter with you?" Charles demanded. "Arthur wanted to take us to the club to see his new boat, the one he built."

"Built?" Madeline's interest was aroused.

"From scratch, in his garage. It took him all winter."

"Really?"

"Want to go down and see it?"

"Okay. I'll get the bikes out." She suddenly felt much better. "Be back soon!" she called to Flash. He hobbled over to her side, and she whispered into his ear, "Thank you."

The Yacht Club was about a mile from the summer house. She and her father used to walk the distance, going down the beaches until they came to the mouth of the harbor. There, enormous rocks covered with slimy moss interrupted their path and forced them through the boatyard to the street. Her father enjoyed the detour because it gave him a chance to admire the giant mushroom anchors, which now lay covered with rust and half-buried in the pebbled sand. "Imagine the size of those ships," he would say, "to need an anchor that big! Just one of them would have filled the whole harbor!"

Charles and Madeline pedaled extra fast.

"Remind me on the way back," Charles said as they passed the library, "to pick up a book on logrolling. I should know *something* about what I'm getting into!"

Madeline was disappointed with Charles for mentioning that unpleasant subject again. "All right," she agreed softly.

They put their bicycles in the rack outside the Junior Clubhouse. Charles hurried down the ramp, having caught sight of Arthur's red head bobbing behind a neat row of small boats turned upside-down on the dock.

"I'll be there in a minute," Madeline called to him, as she hurried up the steps onto the porch. "I'm going into the Junior Clubhouse for a minute!"

The main room of the Clubhouse was filled with worn-out overstuffed furniture that people had donated. Madeline noticed, however, that new drapes were up, and the rickety old piano had a new cushioned seat. A few rugs were scattered around the floor and some folding chairs were lined up along one wall. On rainy days, when it was too bad to sail, the classes were held indoors, and the instructors kept them all busy tying knots or being lectured on racing strategy. Madeline was sure the instructors hated those days as much as the classes did! She was especially glad to see that the old wicker couch along the back wall had had a fresh coat of bright-green paint. The couch was Madeline's favorite, and she and Lisa always made sure that they reached it first.

Madeline went into the dressing room beyond the couch. She combed her hair and splashed water on her face. Then she pinched her cheeks hard, the way Lisa had taught her to do, so they had a pink glow.

When Madeline reached Arthur's boat, she couldn't believe her eyes. She walked up and down the dock, checking it out. The boat was approximately fifteen feet long. Broad and flat as a bathtub in the center and in the stern, its bow tapered to a sharp point which, Arthur explained gravely, enabled the boat to cut effectively through even the roughest waters. Across the center, just below the oarlocks, stretched a wide, polished board. The oarlocks were shiny brass, which looked slightly out of place against the drab-gray of the rail. There was another wide, gleaming board settled across the stern, directly in front of a shiny, freshly painted motor. A skinny board crossed the end of the bow, like glasses across a nose. The slatted floorboards could be removed and used as surfboards outside the harbor, and clearly anyone who disliked wet feet was not welcomed aboard. Water sloshed back and forth beneath the boards. Proudly, large bright-green letters across the stern pronounced this boat *The Admiral.* All in all, it was quite something!

Try as she might, she couldn't suppress her giggles.

"Something funny?" Arthur asked wryly. "Not up to your standards?" He took on a snobbish tone. "Well, then, come aboard, your highness!" He held out his hand to her. Madeline stiffened. "What's the matter? You don't like *The Admiral?*"

"Oh, no, it isn't that."

"Then, come aboard. Let's see what happens."

Charles plunked her down on the middle seat. It was slippery. His fingers pinched her arm, and Madeline got his message.

"By the way, better put these on." Arthur handed them each a life jacket. "Just in case—" He pulled the cord, and the motor started immediately.

"Where did you get the pattern?" Madeline asked.

"Lord, it's not a dress, Madeline," Charles said, laughing.

"Never mind. I *did* have a pattern, as a matter of fact."

"See, smart Charles."

"The boat was an old wreck in the boatyard. I rebuilt the hull."

The day was bright. There were no clouds in the sky, and the harbor water was as smooth as glass.

"Look at that!" Arthur announced proudly, as he pointed off the stern of the boat. "We have a wake!" Madeline clapped. A faint track of ripples was following them. "We are speeding along at an amazing nine knots!"

"Wow!"

Most of the yachts had already left their moorings for a weekend on the Sound, so Arthur had clear space for a perfect test run.

"You know what, Arthur," Madeline said, "I bet you'd make a good sailor."

"So my father wishes!"

Charles nodded to Madeline, urging her on.

"Did anybody ever ask you to crew for them? I mean, would you like to crew. . . would you like to crew for me sometimes, since Charles is going away. . .?" They had reached the end of the harbor and were heading back.

"I might—to please my father. It would quiet him down. He thinks all motorboat people are jerks, and all sailors are pure. Sound familiar?"

"It sure does. Dad always thought motorboats were disgusting. All that ugly gas and oil messing up our clear, blue water."

They all laughed at that as they glanced down into the murky depths. Long Island Sound had never been noted for clear, blue water.

"I'd be a poor substitute for old Charles here, though."

Charles agreed—thumbs up! "I've got to hand it to you, Arthur. Except for a little water seeping into the bow here, she's perfectly seaworthy and—"

It happened fast, directly in front of the Senior Clubhouse. The bow swamped as one of the boards gave way. Charles's last words gurgled noisily to the surface as his head splashed under.

"Yuck!" cried Madeline, laughing so hard that her mouth filled with water, and she almost choked.

Stalwart in the stern, Arthur went down with his ship, as the Captain should.

The club launch was dispatched immediately to save them and found them floating on their backs in a sea of bubbles shouting, "What a great way to start the summer!"

"Maybe I *should* switch to sailing!" Arthur said.

The three of them agreed that *The Admiral* needed more work, and Charles and Arthur, plus the launchmen, would have to spend the rest of the afternoon raising her from the bottom of the harbor.

Madeline decided to go home. She didn't want Arthur to see her looking such a mess, now that he was going to sail with her. His boat might be a piece of junk, but he was more fun than she had remembered. "Thanks for the ride, Arthur!" she called behind her giggling. "I'll bring towels next time! And don't forget to stop at the library, Charles."

She climbed onto her bicycle. Glancing back, she saw them wrestling with a block and tackle down the dock and into the club launch. Oh, well, Madeline knew that they would raise *The Admiral* and that *The Admiral* would float again. Arthur had fixed her once and he would fix her once more.

"See you later!" she called.

Soaked, sticky, and feeling sensational, Madeline pedaled toward home. Her mother had promised her that it would be all right this summer, and her mother had never broken a promise. Nobody felt sorry for her—at least, not today. And it wasn't too hard to be happy again. She pedaled faster. She wanted to get home in a hurry to see her mother, and she wanted to tell her how sorry she was about last night.

July

OTHER
SAILORS

WHEN Madeline arrived at the summer house, Aunt Ede and her mother were sitting on the front porch. Aunt Ede was leaning forward in the bamboo chair. She was dressed in her Saturday clothes: faded slacks and a checkered shirt. Except for the oversized glasses nestled in her hair and the intent, serious expression on her face, she could have been going to a square dance. Madeline's mother was slumped in the matching rocker, a worried expression on her face. Her hair was pulled back and, to Madeline, she looked frighteningly young and hurt—the way she had looked that night last summer, when shock had propelled pain. Madeline's elation vanished quickly as she slipped silently up the stairs and into her room. "They're talking about me," she whispered. "I know they are! Mom is telling Aunt Ede how mean I was to her last night and all those awful things I said."

"Hey Madeline!" Lisa's voice trilled up the stairs. "Can I borrow your bike?"

Damn Lisa! Now her mother would know she was home. Just because Lisa's too lazy to get her own bike out of the garage!

" Okay," Madeline called, as quietly as she could. "*Merci!*"

Madeline walked over to the window. There goes Lisa, stuffed into those tight French blue jeans and that French T–shirt. "I bet she's got the longest legs in Southport and the biggest—"

"Mad, you're back? Come on down, please, and help us! We need your advice on Flash!" her mother called.

Madeline started. "Is Flash all right?" she called down the stairs.

"Yes, of course. Aunt Ede and I are discussing his future."

Maybe her mother wasn't mad, she thought. Maybe she had forgotten about last night. "I'll be right down, Mom—just as soon as I change my clothes!"

Madeline dressed herself quickly and ran down to the porch. She smiled hesitantly at her mother and broadly at Aunt Ede. Crouching on the narrow step, she watched her mother's expression for some sign.

"Aunt Ede's worried about Flash. What's he going to do all summer? He can't swim anymore, and he won't have a boat he can sail in—" She gave Madeline a faint smile.

Aunt Ede leaned forward in her chair and shook her head. "I think Flash should have a boat, princess. What do you think?"

Madeline looked up at her mother. She wondered if her mother had told Aunt Ede about last night. A warm smile greeted Madeline's glance. "Yes, I guess maybe he should," Madeline agreed.

She stood up and walked toward Flash who was asleep by the front door. "Would you like your very own boat, Flash?" Flash wagged his tail slowly. "I'd help you sail it," Madeline went on as she knelt down beside him. "And we could keep her at Aunt Ede's dock over there, where you could keep an eye on her and be ready to go for a sail." Flash struggled to his feet, and his tail wagged faster.

Madeline turned to Aunt Ede and her mother. "Oh, he would like it," she said. "He would like a boat."

She walked over to her mother. "Mom, could I talk to you?"

"Of course, Mad."

Aunt Ede stood up and stretched. "Enough loafing—I have to start supper. See you both later!" She blew them a kiss.

Madeline and her mother walked leisurely across the yard and sat down on the seawall, kicking off their shoes and dangling their legs above the beach. It was late afternoon and a crescent moon had already appeared in the sky, pulling the tide toward shore. Little by little the sandbars were disappearing and the tiny sea urchins were scurrying about, burying themselves again in the mud. The surface of the seawall felt rough against their legs. Yielding to the repeated pounding of strong waves, the cement had cracked in various places, and the grass beside the wall was a solid line of brown, defeated long ago by the salt-spray showers. How angry the sea must get, Madeline thought, when something like this tries to stop it! And she imagined it spitting furiously at the obstacle.

"Mom, I'm so sorry about last night," she began, nervous and embarrassed. "I didn't mean any of those things I said."

"I know, Mad. I understand."

"I love you, Mom. I really do. And I'll change if you want me to. I'll try to be happy. I was today—" and she told her mother all about *The Admiral*.

"I know you'll be happy, Madeline. That's the only change I want." She gave Madeline a hug. "What kind of boat do you think Flash would like?"

"Well, let me think."

Her mother jumped down onto the beach. "Shall we check out some boats tomorrow?"

"I guess we'd better—before Charles goes.

Charles will have to approve our choice," Madeline said. "And, I guess I'd better have an adequate and trustworthy crew to help Flash and me."

"I guess you'd better," her mother agreed.

"Should I ask Arthur and Tory and Lee to come with us?"

"And Lisa," added her mother.

"Our figurehead," Madeline laughed. She turned around. Flash was whimpering and straining with his paws on the seawall.

Her mother nodded happily. "Maybe we should make a path for him through the wall," she suggested, changing the subject.

"It's better this way," Madeline said, helping him over and onto the beach. "This way, he can't chase the swans when we're not looking."

That night, when Madeline went to bed, she drifted off to sleep thinking about having a boat at Aunt Ede's dock again. It didn't matter to her that Aunt Ede and her mother had planned the boat around Flash. It didn't matter to her that her mother had probably told Aunt Ede all about last night. She had already decided to get a boat for Aunt Ede's dock, and she had already decided to see her friends again. That's what her father would have wanted. Bells tinkled lazily in the distance, and the waves stroked the beach. A flutter of wind stirred the curtains, and the warm, peaceful night enveloped her room.

"We'll pick you up after church, Arthur. Charles told me to call you. Okay?"

"Calling Arthur, huh?" Lisa swept through the door. Madeline wondered why Lisa never walked. She either "swept" or "swung." She was wearing Mrs. Davis's kind of wide-brimmed straw hat. "What are we doing after church?"

"Buying a boat," Madeline answered bluntly.

Merveilleux! But I can't make it! I have a sailing date!" She put her finger to her tongue; then extended it above her hat. "I believe the wind is southwest by ten knots—perfect!"

"You're off six knots and your direction is wrong," Charles corrected her as he opened the door. "Grandmother said to hurry up!"

As they entered the church, the narthex was crowded with people. Madeline felt a painful sensation in the back of her throat. Last August the narthex was crowded with people, too, but then, the air was still and heavy with floral perfumes. The people weren't smiling, and their voices were soft and sad. Today, Madeline felt self-conscious, as her mother led the way down the aisle to their usual pew. Aunt Ede followed her mother. Everyone seemed to be looking at them, which pleased Lisa immensely. Lisa walked down the aisle like a bride every Sunday. Madeline hated sitting next to her in church. She crossed her legs tidily during the scriptures, until they resembled the long parallel ribbons on her hat. And she always whispered the Lord's Prayer in French!

Madeline's father had not gone to church often. "My surroundings are my church," he had always said, "wherever I am. What difference does a building make?"

"A building gives religion a home, a structured feeling, something tangible," her mother had insisted. "That's important to a child. A child can't cope with concepts," her mother had added.

"All right, my darling, Madeline shall go to church," her father had said with a laugh. "But I'll get to heaven too. Don't you be surprised!"

In New York, church was a cathedral, with its towering spires, like giant antennae catching waves transmitted from heaven; but in Southport, church was a simple colonial building with one not-so-tall steeple that always seemed to need painting and housed a bell whose sound was the slightest bit off-pitch. Madeline guessed her father was probably right. Church was where you were and how you felt at any given moment. Exactly like that last day on *The Great Lady.* She and her father had been in church that day, together.

Madeline saw Mrs. Davis on the lawn after the service. Mrs. Davis looked like a snowman from the back in her white skirt and blouse. She was a stack of circles. "Hi, Mrs. Davis!" Madeline called.

Mrs. Davis hurried over with her cup of lemonade. "Just who I want to see!" she bellowed. "I have the boat for you, honey! Saw her yesterday. In the boatyard over by Sasco Hill."

"As a matter of fact," Madeline started, "we plan to—"

"This is the one!" Mrs. Davis insisted. "The same man who bought *The Great Lady*—it's *his* boat. He wanted a bigger one!"

Madeline felt strange. She tried to smile.

"Well, you want a smaller one." Mrs. Davis clapped her hands, and the straw hat bounced on her head. "Sort of a trade."

Madeline hesitated. "Many thanks," she said. "We'll certainly look at her."

Lisa came up behind Madeline and nudged her. "We've got to go!" Lisa gave Mrs. Davis a warm smile and kissed her lightly on the cheek.

"Hey, there, Lisa, take off my hat!" Mrs. Davis joked. She squeezed Lisa's hand. "Well," she sighed heavily, "you look better in it, anyway!"

Madeline had to agree with that.

The Sasco Hill boatyard was one of the oldest boatyards in the area, and Madeline's father had always considered a trip there a special treat. The new boats filled one whole side of the loading tracks, which snaked from the water, up the ramp, across the gravel and sand and dust, and into the shed. The boats stood in neat, sparkling rows on trailers, displayed in finest fashion. But the other side of the loading tracks was in constant disarray with derelicts and antique hulls. That side was the fun side, where you could always find some treasure, either by climbing up a ladder to peer inside some long-abandoned cabin, or by checking through some rusty barrel, or even by just wandering along some rickety old dock, swaying on its rotted pilings. The scaffolding and cranes that towered above the long one-story shed looked like awesome fingers pointing to where new boats were actually assembled to sell. The shed smelled of new rope and glue and marine paint and varnish and hot fiber glass melts and molds—"good smells," Madeline's father had said.

The boat Mrs. Davis had recommended to Madeline was still afloat on the other side of the shed near the ramp that slid underwater. The boat was called *The Lady*—for the seller's daughter, a man at the boat yard told them. The daughter was married now and had moved to a small town in the midwest where the lakes don't welcome twenty-four foot sloops. He had sailed her himself off the coast of Maine, but now he and his wife wanted to cruise south in *The Great Lady*.

"Where is she now?" Madeline asked the man, "*The Great Lady*, I mean. I didn't see her at the club yesterday."

"Oh, he sailed *her* back to Maine. She probably won't be this way again until August."

Madeline felt a twinge. She climbed aboard *The Lady*.

Tory and Lee were already on board, examining the heavily varnished rail and mast as the boat rocked gently from side to side.

"There's the greatest cabin fore!" Tory exclaimed.

"Really great!" agreed Lee.

"Sleeps two people in there."

"Imagine two *real* bunks!"

Arthur had positioned himself predictably at the engine box aft and had taken the lid off. Charles was busy inspecting the hull.

Madeline's eyes examined every inch of the boat. Running parallel below the rail behind the cabin area was a continuous wide seat from port to stern to starboard, which meant the skipper could sit anywhere on the boat and, without even getting up, maneuver easily around to change a course. The long tiller, extending like a giant arm from the stern, accommodated the skipper's flexibility. Inside the cabin were two wide boards, reaching to a *V* in the bow. Those were the bunks, covered with waterproof cushions. Madeline ducked in and stretched out on one side. She fit perfectly.

As she climbed back on shore, her eyes scanned it all—from the masthead to the rails. Madeline could tell the boat had been cared for and loved very much. The man's daughter had probably been heartbroken to have to lose her.

"Well," Madeline called, "what do you think, Mom? Do you like her?"

Her mother and Aunt Ede were talking by the car. "Well, she sort of already *is* in the family, isn't she?"

Madeline smiled broadly.

Charles made the decision. He and Madeline had concluded ahead of time that it was up to Charles, who was more exacting. "She's what you want," he declared. "I've checked her through."

Madeline didn't hesitate. She had a most positive feeling.

"You know, Mom," she said at supper that night, "it's almost as if Dad can somehow *make* things happen. I mean, as if he plans things." She was concentrating hard. "With that particular boat being there—just the *right* kind of boat, and having belonged to that particular man . . ." Her voice trailed off.

"Well, there're nice things that happen."

"He always said that he'd watch over us," Madeline went on. "But I miss him, Mom. Like today."

Her mother put her arms around Madeline. "But he was there, don't you think?"

"Yes," Madeline said, and she knew that it was true.

The next morning she was up early, dressed in her oldest blue jeans and a faded striped shirt. It was essential to look exactly right on the first day of sailing class. She slipped into last year's Docksider shoes, which had broken-down backs and laces raveling out at the ends and were a little too small. After examining herself carefully in the mirror, she smiled. She looked fine—just like a native. Shaking out her hair, she gathered it in a ponytail. Pulled out straight, it was almost as long as Lisa's, but it always sprang back up. Why did she have to have curly hair?

"Hey, Madeline, hurry up," Lisa called across the driveway. "Let's go!" Lisa was perched on Charles's bicycle.

"Where's Charles?"

"He is staying home to receive *The Lady* when she arrives," Lisa answered. "Besides, he's not taking the classes this year, remember? Come on!"

Madeline knew Lisa was in a hurry to meet the new sailing instructors. They were always college boys, and Lisa liked college boys. Girls brought up in Europe are consistently more mature, she maintained. Lisa was dressed for the occasion in lavendar slacks and a maroon halter. She was going to look awful when she got wet, Madeline mused.

"Lisa, you can't go sailing in sandals," Madeline reminded her, as they rode along.

"Since when do we go sailing on the first day of class? This is get-acquainted day—always has been." Lisa's hair waved like a flag behind her. *"Mon jour favori!"*

Standing in the middle of the parking lot above the docks, Douglas McAllister was surrounded by hordes of confused little children and inquiring adults. He was well over six-feet tall, with curly blond hair and bright-blue eyes, and he had a deep tan, probably left over from a winter of skiing. He resembled one of her father's Greek gods, peering down at his people during battle. Madeline felt intimidated just looking at him. She hoped that he wouldn't notice her. At once she wanted Lisa to quickly disappear. Without Lisa beside her, he would *never* notice her. But at the same time she wanted Lisa to stay so she wouldn't feel so alone. She suddenly felt really sick to her stomach and wanted to hide—the way she had felt that first day when she had hidden from Arthur in the bottom of the car. I wish I were at the bottom of the harbor, she said to herself.

"Mon Dieu!" cried Lisa, squeezing by the crowd and putting her bicycle in the rack. *"Cet pauvre homme!"* She quickly smoothed out her hair and swung to his side. Douglas McAllister welcomed her with a wide, white smile. *"Venez! Venez!"* Lisa directed. Then, realizing that no one was understanding her, and having made her impression,

she slipped into English: "Come! Come!" Soon everyone was lined up, and a chaotic signing-in process was under control. Douglas McAllister was extremely grateful. His goddess had arrived.

Madeline felt awkward and alone. Why did she get a stomachache around new people? She wished she hadn't come today. She wasn't any good at getting acquainted, not the way Lisa was.

"Hi, Madeline." It was Arthur. She didn't even want to see Arthur, not now. "Want to help me get some boats in the water? I see your cousin is busy elsewhere," he said, motioning toward Lisa.

"Oh, no thanks, Arthur. Maybe later." Her stomach cramps were getting worse. "I just came down for a minute." She wanted to go home. She didn't want Arthur trying to be nice to her, feeling sorry for her. "I'll see you later." She hurriedly climbed on her bike.

"Hey! Aren't you going sailing?"

She took a deep breath and it hurt her chest. "Nobody sails the first day of class! This is get-acquainted day—always has been!" Tears filled her eyes, and she pedaled as fast as she could for home.

Riding through the gate, she saw that *The Lady* had already been delivered and was rocking comfortably at Aunt Ede's dock, as if she belonged there, tugging gently on her lines, pleased to be home. Charles had stepped the mast and raised the sails. He had even placed a flag on the staff. Madeline stepped off her bike and stood staring at her new boat. She had an odd sensation, and the tears began to trickle down her cheeks. It was last summer, and she was going sailing with her father. She could almost see him standing on the foredeck as the late-August sun winked through Aunt Ede's trees. He would call her in a minute to hurry up for "the best wind we've had all summer!"

"Madeline! You're home! Isn't she great!" Charles came leaping out of Aunt Ede's kitchen door. "Let's take her out!" Madeline brushed her face quickly with her hand so Charles wouldn't see that she had been crying. "How come you're not in class?"

"There's nothing to do down there today. You know, things don't get started till tomorrow."

Charles grabbed her hand. *"All right!* Let's go!" They ran across the yard. "You know, now I wish I weren't going away for the summer!"

"I wish you weren't either," Madeline said, but Charles didn't hear her. He was ahead of her, already on the boat.

"Untie that line," he told Madeline. "Let's go!"

"Hey, Charles, wait for me." She tossed the line into the stern and jumped aboard just in time.

Charles let the sail fill, and Madeline grabbed the tiller.

"Hey, she's great!" Charles called behind him. "Smooth as anything!"

They sailed *The Lady* up the harbor and into a vacant slip by the Senior Clubhouse.

"Lord," Charles remarked, looking toward the

Junior docks, "there are an awful lot of kids this year."

"Fifty-eight," Madeline said with a shudder, "and most of them new and *young.*"

"The five of you old people are going to be busy helping all the instructors. All those beginning sailors—"

"Yuck."

"Hey, Arthur, over here!" Charles climbed up on the rail. "Madeline's new boat!"

Arthur was tipping the small boats into the water and clearing the dock space. He hurried over to *The Lady.*

"All right!" he exclaimed as he jumped aboard.

"Where's my sister?" Charles asked.

Arthur pointed behind a hoist that was holding a boat suspended over the water. Lisa was barefoot now and had wound her hair in a loop on top of her head. She referred to that style as her businesslike image. Close beside her stood Douglas McAllister, guiding the boat as she worked the buttons.

"Can't anyone get Miss France afloat?" Charles asked.

Arthur and Madeline laughed.

"Where are Tory and Lee?" Charles asked.

"This is Greenfield Hill day—tennis, swimming, and riding," Madeline recited. "Tory promised that they would be here tomorrow."

"Well, in that case let's us sail back home and get

some lunch," Charles suggested. "Who wants to stand in a long line today for food with all these kids around?"

"Great idea. I'll tell Doug we'll be back," Arthur said.

Flash was lying on Aunt Ede's dock, stretched out, asleep in the sun.

"Flash!" Madeline called from the deck, as they headed in. "What do you think of *The Lady?*" Flash looked up and wagged his tail, but he didn't stand.

Arthur jumped out and secured the bow line while Charles cleated a line near the stern. The two of them disappeared across the lawn.

Madeline jumped on the dock next to Flash. She sat down and put his head in her lap. "Oh, you're mad at me, aren't you, 'cause we didn't take you out on the boat. And it's your boat, too." She stroked his back. "Well, I'll take you for a sail this afternoon, as soon as I come back from class. I promise." She held his head up to her face. "And we didn't mean to leave you behind. Honest. It's just that we were so excited and left in such a hurry, and you weren't around." She kissed his nose. "I love you, Flash." As she stood, she motioned for him to follow. "Come on, let's get some lunch!" But when Madeline looked back, she saw that he was having trouble standing. "Poor Flash, you stay right there. I'll bring you your lunch on the dock."

Charles and Arthur were in Aunt Ede's kitchen. Madeline could hear them through the window. She ran on into the summer house.

"How's *The Lady*?" her mother called, following Madeline upstairs.

"Oh, she's great, Mom. She really is! Mom, what did Flash do today? He seems awfully tired."

"He was with me down by the sea wall," her mother answered. "I was painting most of the morning. There was an extraordinary swan way out on the water. I sketched him in and thought I'd build a picture around him."

Madeline wasn't particularly interested in the subject of her mother's latest painting at the moment. "Well, did Flash go swimming or anything? Why is he so tired acting?"

"I don't know, Mad. Flash is getting on in years. He's not the same puppy you once had."

"Now you're sounding just like Charles. Telling me that Flash is going to die or something. Well he isn't. I'll see to it."

"I'm not telling you anything, Madeline, except not to expect too much of him any more. That's all."

Madeline turned sharply, grabbed a handful of dog biscuits and hurried out the door. "I'm feeding him lunch on the dock today."

July was the best month of all, Madeline decided. In June, the cold water lingered on, and, if your boat happened to capsize, the water gave you a terrible chill. In August, if you fell overboard, the jellyfish gave you a terrible sting. So that left July—clear, hot and wonderful.

As the Blue Jays clustered around the committee boat, waiting for the July Fourth races to start, Madeline let go of the tiller in order to feel the tide-drift. Arthur had already slacked off on the mainsheet. The committee boat was an oversized motor launch that served several purposes: it set the course for the races, timed the races, and was available to any boat in trouble. It was also a refreshment stand, stocked with cold sodas and bags of grapes. Grapes were better than sodas if anyone were really thirsty. The instructors also taught sailing from its bow, their voices booming over megaphones.

"The tide will make a big difference today," Madeline said. "Look at this!" *Banana Peel* swooped sideways. "We'll have to compensate for that current. Let's tack to starboard." Arthur shifted his weight to the other side.

Getting a good start in a race was essential. Madeline's father had taught her his motto long ago: How you start is how you finish. And he had usually been the first boat across the starting line.

"We shouldn't get too far from the committee boat," Arthur warned her. Arthur might be crew, but he had spent two years on the committee boat, running the races, and she respected his opinion.

Today, Douglas McAllister, Lisa, and Charles were running the race.

The whistle sounded for the two-minute warning.

"Not so far downwind!" Douglas McAllister shouted through his megaphone. Madeline looked around. He was calling to Lee.

"What's Lee doing way over there?"

"Probably having problems with her crew," Arthur answered. "Where's Tory?"

"Tory never came today. She stayed for some horse show," Madeline said. Charles was right. Tory was overbooked in summer activities. Now, if Madeline weren't too bossy and didn't make Arthur mad, she would probably have the best crew in her class.

"There are eight boats today," Arthur counted. "That's more than usual."

"Because it's a perfect day!" Madeline exclaimed, as the minute-and-a-half warning came. "Come about!" The boat tacked quickly. "For a motorboat type, you're pretty smart!"

"Well, after all, I *did* sail with your father," Arthur reminded her, with a smile. "I'm not all bad."

Charles blew the whistle for thirty seconds. "You look great!" he called to them.

And they were—right on target. At the starting gun, they crossed the line a good twelve seconds before any other boat.

Lisa and Charles waved wildly, and Douglas

McAllister shouted, "Good work!" after them. Lisa looked every bit like Mrs. Charles de Gaulle in the presidential box.

Heading for the first mark, they had clear wind and a close-hauled course. As the committee boat grew tiny behind them, Madeline held the tiller with confidence. She was relaxed. "Might as well cleat the mainsheet," she told Arthur. "I hope you don't mind crewing for me."

"Not if we win!" he assured her.

"And you don't mind sailing?"

"Not today."

"It's always great," Madeline went on. "Never the same. Unpredictable, I guess that's the word. Not like a motorboat."

"*My* motorboats are unpredictable!"

They both laughed.

As they rounded the last mark, Lee came close enough so they could yell back and forth. The other boats were still far behind.

"Keep your distance!" shouted Arthur.

Lee was hunched down at the tiller with a determined look on her face. Her crew, a younger girl, was sitting on the rail, hanging off the side, looking helpless and scared.

"Lee!" shouted Madeline, "you're going to capsize!"

And she did, just before *Banana Peel* crossed the finish line.

Charles started the engine on the committee boat and Lisa threw Madeline and Arthur a bag of grapes as they headed out to pick up Lee.

"Quel dommage!" Madeline heard Lisa wail, as they speeded away.

Arthur was munching on grapes. "You know, Madeline, your father used to tell me how great you were. *I* thought you were stuck up."

Madeline smiled. "You mean like Lisa?"

"Oh, no. Not as bad as Lisa. But you *did* always act like you thought you were better, more sophisticated, than us country folk, even when we were little. You were never friendly, like Charles." Madeline frowned as Arthur bumbled on: "Please don't get mad at me for saying it." She didn't know what to answer. Arthur was out of character, too personal. "Would you let me buy you a pizza tonight? Since Charles leaves for Oregon tomorrow, and since we won the race today—I mean, *you* won the race today. I'll ask Charles too," he quickly added.

Madeline relaxed when she heard Charles was included in the plans. "Okay. Fine. I'd like to." She focused on the tiller again, trying to remain calm—as Arthur had put it—"sophisticated". She felt terribly flushed and excited.

The six other Blue Jays crossed the finish line in rapid succession. Behind them, the committee boat returned with a dripping, giggling Lee and her sputtering, quivering crew, in addition to its original team.

As Madeline and Arthur led the procession back into the harbor, the sun blinked brightly behind the clouds, and, just for a moment, Madeline felt the most wonderful warm wind touch her face.

MIDSUMMER NIGHTS

FLASH lay on the rug beside Madeline's bed.

"How do I look, kind sir?" she asked him. Flash glanced up at her for an instant and then dropped his head back down. "You're still mad at me, aren't you?" She knelt down beside him. "Oh, I know! I forgot! Oh, Flash, I'm so sorry. I promised you we'd go sailing, and then I forgot!" Flash cocked an eye at her. "Oh, please forgive me! That was awful! And now I'm going off and leaving you tonight." Flash closed his eyes again. "I really don't like Arthur better then you. I promise I don't." She hugged him hard. "I love you most of all." Then she stood up and added, "Tomorrow will be *our* day!"

"Madeline!" her mother's voice resounded up the stairs. "Arthur's here!"

Madeline suddenly felt sick to her stomach, the way she had felt that morning when Lisa had left her alone at the Yacht Club. "Is Charles here?" she called, but no one answered. Being alone with Arthur on a boat wasn't bad. But, being alone with him on a date—the very word made her shudder—was something else. What ever would she say? Boys always expected girls to entertain them, Lisa said. Madeline felt panicked as she stared at herself in the mirror. She didn't look very entertaining—in fact, she looked dead! White sandals, white pants, white shirt, white face, white hair! And Flash was no help. He was ignoring her!

"Madeline, did you hear me?" her mother called again. "Arthur's here!"

"Yes, Mom, I'll be right down."

She studied herself in the mirror. That's what was wrong! She was all one color! Quickly taking off the white shirt, she changed into a blue one, then looked in the mirror again. Much better! The blue shirt didn't look so tight, and it matched her eyes. She hugged Flash. "I wish I could stay home with you tonight."

As she started down the stairs, a terrible thought occurred to her: eating pizza in white pants! Yuck! Lisa would never eat pizza in public at all! But it was too late!

"Hi, Madeline." Arthur handed her a yellow rose. "I passed Mrs. Chapman's house on the way." Poor Arthur had had a long walk. He lived near the Yacht

Club in the center of the village. Now he had to walk all the way back. She should have met him there. Now she would have to entertain him all the way back. She thought again of Lisa and stuck the rose in one side of her hair.

"Bye, Mom. See you later."

"Have fun!" her mother replied, smiling at them both as they went out the door. Aunt Ede and her mother were going to a movie. Madeline wished she could go with them.

"Where's Charles?" she asked, hesitantly.

"He's meeting us there."

Please, God, thought Madeline. Let Charles be there.

"Remember, Madeline, when we were little and had the secret club?" Arthur spoke very precisely, as if he had memorized a list for conversation.

Madeline smiled. "Yes—in Aunt Ede's basement. It was all musty down there, and it smelled. I remember. You kept all the notes and the schedules."

"A most important job," Arthur said, laughing, "like Lee's important job of picking up the order at the Candy Kitchen: four Hershey bars, three grape bubble gums, two orange sodas—"

"And one apple juice," Madeline added. "Just to complicate the order." Madeline shook her head. "Lisa always had to be a little different." Her tone grew serious. "Arthur, do boys like Lisa?"

"No. I don't think so. Why?"

"Oh, I don't know. I was just wondering."

"Well, she *is* pretty and—well, I guess she's fun at times, but, I don't know—you can't really talk to her and be friends with her."

Madeline shrugged. "Oh, well, I just meant she always has boys following her around."

"That doesn't mean they especially like her." Madeline's eyes widened in surprise. "They just like the way she looks. Besides, I don't think she has a thought in her head—I mean an important thought. I could never really talk to her *at all* about anything—you know—serious. She just flips her head, gives you that silly smile, and says something stupid in French." He summed it up: "I think she's phony."

Madeline hesitated for a moment and then dropped the subject. She shouldn't have brought it up. "When we started sailing classes that summer, all together—that's what I remember the best."

Arthur responded with a laugh almost too loud. "All we ever did was fall out of those little nine-foot boats."

"Remember how Lisa cried every time she got her hair wet because Tory told her that salt water can make you go bald?" There she was talking about Lisa again.

"And I told Lisa that she was always too stuck up?"

"Sophisticated," Madeline corrected him.

"And remember when your father took us all on an overnight cruise and we slept on the boat? That was the first time Lee had ever been away from home overnight, and Charles told her that a huge whale was loose in the Sound."

"And Charles put a dead fish in Lisa's sleeping bag."

They both laughed. "Remember last year when we had that fight with the water balloons and nearly swamped Tory?"

Madeline clapped her hands. "And that wonderful time you took your mother out in your first homemade boat. She had just had her hair curled, and the boat capsized—"

"The All-American Jerk!" he said, imitating his father's deep, solemn voice.

Madeline wondered what they would talk about when they ran out of things to remember. She walked along briskly, anxious to join Charles. The sun was shaded by the hills now, and the village streets were almost deserted. At this time, the city streets would be dizzy with people rushing to evening haunts that never closed. A few times within the last several years her parents had taken her to a nightclub, dazzling with lights and waiters in stiff-collared evening wear. They had sat quietly, listening to the orchestra, and there had never been a need to make sparkling conversation. She had always felt so comfortable with her parents when they had gone out for an evening. But, oh, tonight—the pizza place seemed miles away.

"How's school?" she asked dully. She knew Arthur had always hated school.

"I like it this year," he answered, much to her surprise. "I have this new course—really interesting."

"Boys like to talk about themselves," Lisa had told her.

She brightened and asked, "What course?"

"Philosophy."

Madeline started to giggle. "I'm sorry, Arthur, I don't mean to laugh. It's just that I never thought of you as a philosopher. I mean, you're a mathematical type." She turned to him.

Arthur smiled. "Oh, that's all right. Now you know my hidden depths."

Charles was waiting for them in a booth just inside the door. Music blasted from a jukebox in the back corner, and the bright lights made Madeline's eyes squint. "Charles, guess what?" she cried nervously, rushing over to him. "Arthur has hidden depths. Isn't it marvelous!" She was relieved to see Charles, but she was clearly embarrassing Arthur. Arthur's face turned the color of his hair.

"Of course. He's *mysterious*," Charles said, grabbing Arthur's arm, reassuringly.

Arthur twirled a nonexistent mustache as he entered into the joke. "You had better forget your mission, Sir Charles, and remain at the castle."

"I think you're right," Charles said seriously. "Come and sit down and I shall read you some great tales of the northwest." He opened the library book. "I don't think I'll survive. I'm not the rugged type."

Madeline tilted her head, looking Charles over carefully. Charles had a square face, like a tic-tac-toe box with the proper frames filled in and eyebrows that wouldn't stop. He was short, but he was strong. He always had been. And he was agile. When they were small, Charles was the one who climbed the beech tree like a monkey and sat on the highest branch like a block. And now, when he crewed for Madeline, he could hike out almost past the sail with the mainsheet in his teeth, even on the windiest day; and back on land, he could lift the mast up and down by himself when it was necessary. Charles said that he had grown strong as he fought his way through Europe, but Lisa said that he was forever lifting weights in his room and running around the school track after classes. Also he crewed for his school's rowing team every spring and fall, and that alone could make your arms bulge.

"Well, you'll have to go now," Arthur said, as he settled in beside Madeline, "because you've lost your summer job."

"I saw you win today—out of eight boats. That's pretty good, little cousin. And you did it without me."

"I had Arthur, and he's every bit as good as you." Madeline smiled and shyly touched Arthur's arm.

She felt calmer and more self-assured, and her stomach didn't hurt anymore. She secretly wondered if all the people in the pizza place were noticing her, talking and smiling and laughing with two great-looking boys.

"What'll you have?" Arthur asked when the waitress stopped by their table.

"I'll have pizza with mushrooms," Madeline answered, realizing suddenly that she was starved.

Charles had Aunt Ede's car, so, after they had eaten, they drove around, passing the old-fashioned movie house and the ice-cream palace in Southport and Arthur's father's bookstore, antique shops, and the department store in the next town. Since Charles was leaving the following day, the after-dinner mood was subdued, and none of them wanted the evening to end.

Charles and Arthur discussed the car's engine pick-up and the brakes and the muffler and the transmission, while Madeline, squeezed between the two of them, thought about the summer. It was going to be all right, just as her mother had promised. She seemed to be all set. Her Blue Jay was still the fastest boat in her class and she had the best crew. *The Lady* had somehow sailed her way, and she wasn't going to be lost when Charles was gone. Arthur seemed really nice, and she had good friends. And most of all, she had Flash to tell her troubles to. She was very lucky.

"It's a beautiful night," she said to Charles, after

they had dropped Arthur off at his house. "Thank you, big cousin. I'm going to be just fine!"

The high point of the Junior social season was the Commodore's Dance. Even though Madeline had never attended one, she had heard the music year after year as it drifted down the water to the summer house. Every year it seemed louder, and there were fewer and fewer pretty melodies. Madeline wondered what all those ladies on Simpson's balconies would have thought of the music today. They could never have danced in their long, flowing dresses, and they probably would have tripped and toppled off the balconies head first, covering their ears with their fans. Last summer her father finally had to close all the windows, and even then, a dull beat still penetrated the walls.

"How do you dance to music like that, anyway?" her father has asked. Even her mother, as young as she was, didn't know.

Madeline showed him. She had seen it on television, and once they had tried it at dancing class in the city. But the class got all mixed up and out of control, and Miss Pryor, the fidgety teacher, had to stop the record in a hurry. Then she quickly resumed her dignified position on the stage, tapping her tiny high-heel shoe against the piano pedal. And *that* was the end of *that* kind of dancing!

"I really don't like it much," Madeline had told her father. "It's kind of stupid-looking."

"Hardly a royal style!" Her father had laughed. "More like an exercise class in the basement of the palace." Then he had swept Madeline and her mother around the porch, humming a Strauss waltz.

"I don't dance to stuff like that," Arthur assured Madeline when he asked her to go to the Commodore's Dance with him. "In fact, I don't dance at all. But if—"

"Oh, that's all right," Madeline interrupted. "I really don't dance either." She thought of the dancing class again. She was always the last girl to be picked when Miss Pryor struck the three chords for the boys to choose their partners. Madeline was taller than the other girls, and her figure was "slow to mature," as the doctor put it. That fact didn't bother the doctor, and it didn't bother Madeline too much, but it seemed to bother the boys in dancing class a great deal. They called her "flatsy" and "stick" and things like that. Madeline called them "perverted." Anyway, there were never enough of them to go around, and when the dreaded three chords shook the room, the few boys who hadn't already left for the men's room ran out in the hallway and disappeared through the exit. Madeline always sat in the back row, obscuring herself methodically behind a bust of Benjamin Franklin.

She was relieved that Arthur didn't dance. "I'd love to go! It will be a lot of fun," she told him.

"Good. That's settled," Arthur announced. "Now let's get *Banana Peel* in the water and win all three races today!"

Flash was lying by the sea wall when Madeline came home. She spotted him from the gate and hurried down the lawn to join him. "Guess what, Flash. I'm going to the big dance! Isn't it wonderful? That's the noisy one, the one that makes you howl!" Flash wagged his tail and licked Madeline's face. "The best part of all is that Arthur doesn't dance either! Isn't it *great?*" Flash dropped his head onto her lap with a snort. "Now, don't be mad at me. I still don't like Arthur better than you. It's just that he asked me first." She jumped up, forcing Flash to his feet. He stood there unsteadily. "Let's celebrate, Flash. Let's go sailing. Come on! Hurry!" And she pulled him up and over to Aunt Ede's dock. He followed her onto the boat and took his place in the stern, just the way he had done on *The Great Lady*.

"Flash is the best mate a captain could ever have," her father had said. "He never corrects the captain and he knows where he belongs." Flash always went with them when they sailed for fun. "All that weight is good ballast!" But, when her father raced, it was "serious sailing." Flash stayed at home, but Madeline was always there.

Just as she raised the mainsail, she saw Lisa and Douglas McAllister appear in the driveway. "We'll have to hurry, Flash, if we want to escape. Wish hard for some wind!" Lisa's long legs were striding toward the dock and Douglas McAllister was fast on her heels.

"Attendez! Attendez!" Lisa called. "Madeline! *Attendez!"*

Suddenly, the wind caught the sail, and the boat surged ahead. Flash let his ears fly free in the breeze. Madeline glanced around and saw Lisa and Douglas McAllister collapsed on the beach.

They tacked out through a flock of swans floating in formation on the water. Madeline was careful not to disturb them, and she managed several neat tacks, zigzagging out of their way.

"I love *The Lady*, don't you, Flash. She's a lot like *The Great Lady*, but she's younger."

Having cleared the swans, she cleated the mainsheet and relaxed, leaning back against Flash. It was late afternoon, and there were no boats on the water. A brisk, steady wind held them on course.

"We're going to have a lot of good sails, you and I. We'll escape Lisa every time. It will be great fun this summer!" She nudged Flash. "We might bring Arthur along sometimes!" Flash wiggled his approval. It was just like old times. The boat slid swiftly through the water, slices of foam streaking behind it, and large clusters of clouds piled high above the mast while a sliver of moon foreshadowed evening. It was a lovely time of day,

Madeline thought, so peaceful and quiet and fulfilled. It was a picture her mother should paint.

"Come about! We're out far enough!" Flash recognized the words and lay down in the bottom of the boat. Madeline pushed the tiller, and they made a perfect tack.

And just in time, too. Off in the distance, Madeline saw a swan, all alone, rising tall in the water. He was huge. What's a swan doing way out here? she wondered. He must be lost. Lucky we turned around. If we had stayed on course, we would have hit him.

"Lisa, what are you wearing to the dance?" Madeline asked her just for laughs. She could imagine what fantastic outfit Lisa had probably dreamed up. But, then again, maybe Douglas McAllister had changed her taste a little. Lately, Lisa was wearing baggy shorts and bulky shirts. She looked halfway normal.

"Are you going?" Lisa's voice hinted surprise. "Who with ?"

"I'm going with Arthur." Madeline almost surprised herself with the proud tone in her answer.

"*Merveilleux!* He's so cute!"

Madeline had never thought of Arthur as particularly cute, but she decided to let that one pass.

"I'm wearing a skirt," Lisa said, "because the

Commodore's Dance sounds important and has a formal ring to it. Don't you agree?" She didn't wait for Madeline to answer. What Madeline thought hardly mattered. "I thought a sundress. Don't you think?" Again no pause. "I look good in sundresses, and they're all the rage in France. Don't you think I look good in sundresses?" Here she paused, because she was interested in hearing Madeline's compliment.

"You look good in sundresses, Lisa," Madeline said in a bored, mechanical way.

"I have to run, *chérie!* Douglas and I are off to the movies!" Douglas McAllister's car pulled into the driveway right on cue. He *would* have a 1940 Ford convertible. "By the way, Madeline, wait for Douglas and me the next time you take Flash for a sail!"

Fat chance! Madeline said to herself. As for what to wear to the dance, she would check with Tory.

Madeline came home early the next day. She and her mother were going shopping. After she had showered and washed her hair, she put on her white pants and blue shirt. Then she checked herself in the mirror. If only she weren't so thin. She would never be able to keep a sundress up the way Lisa did. She would have to wear one with shoulder straps like little babies on the beach.

"Are you ready, Mad?" her mother called. "It'll take us a half-hour to get there."

They were going to Aunt Ede's favorite store, a few towns down the turnpike. It was a New York store with a suburban branch in Stamford.

"It's funny," Madeline said, "I've never even been in the main store in the city." Madeline wore a uniform to school and the few times she needed a dress for dancing class or concerts or plays, her mother found something at a little shop next door to the apartment building. Her mother had excellent taste, and Madeline wasn't fussy. Buying clothes was a waste of time. She much preferred going to the marine store with her father.

"What color sundress do you want?" her mother asked as they drove along.

Madeline was definite. "Anything but *blue*. Everything I own is *blue*."

"Well, I'm sure we'll find something just right. We'll have plenty of choices."

The teen-age shop, on the second floor, was alive with color. Amplified music pounded against the walls and bounced back and forth between the doors. Madeline looked around. There were things all over the place—on hangers, on counters, on shelves, in glass cases. A feeling of panic gripped her as the noise and the crush of clothes and people closed in. There were too many choices. It would take too long to decide. She began to perspire.

"What if I see someone I know?" she whispered to her mother. The color left her face. People were hurrying back and forth, in and out of cubicles, carrying stacks of clothes. She stood transfixed, staring at people who were staring at clothes. So many people. She began to perspire even more.

"Madeline! Over here! Here are the sundresses!" Oh, she wished her mother wouldn't call to her. She felt so obvious.

"Oh, not white," she agonized, remembering herself as all one color.

"Here's a pretty red one," her mother suggested.

"Oh, not red! It looks so hot!" She was perspiring unmercifully.

Her mother's voice sounded a bit on edge. "Madeline, maybe if you looked at the clothes, instead of looking at the people—"

Oh, why did her mother call her name again. Suddenly: "I want blue." She took command of herself. "Blue is my favorite color."

Her mother picked through the tickets for Madeline's size. Triumphantly, she pulled out a blue sundress. "You should try it on. I'll find someone who—"

"Oh, I *can't* try it on *here*," Madeline whispered. "I smell. I know I smell. I'm so hot. *Please*, couldn't we just take it home. I'll try it on there."

Her mother took the dress over to a woman behind a counter. "We'd like to take this out on approval," Madeline heard her say. "If it isn't right, we'll bring it back tomorrow."

Madeline hurried to the elevator. She and her mother both knew, without saying a word, that the dress would be right—no matter what. They were not coming back tomorrow.

"I think I made a very good choice," Madeline said as she sank, exhausted, into the car. "That was fun! Thank you, Mom. I really enjoyed this afternoon." She leaned over and gave her mother a kiss on the cheek.

"How about shoes?" her mother asked, hesitantly, as she started the car.

"Oh, I have shoes to wear," Madeline assured her. "Besides, Tory said the girls usually dance in bare feet."

Madeline's mother sighed in relief. "That's good," she said, and she turned the car toward home.

Madeline couldn't sleep that night. She finally went downstairs and fixed herself some warm milk. Flash joined her for a cookie.

"You know, Flash, I'm not so sure I want to go to the dance tomorrow night. Oh, I know Lisa goes every year. And she says it's a lot of fun." She glanced over toward Aunt Ede's house. The house was dark. Naturally, Lisa was sleeping soundly, and she would wake up tomorrow refreshed and beautiful. "But I'm not like Lisa." Flash nuzzled her arm. "You're nice to say that—but, sometimes I wish I were." She broke off another piece of the cookie and gave it to him. "Like the time she came in dead-last in all three races that afternoon, when she finally went out in a boat, and she made it more important than coming in first." Madeline frowned. "You know, Douglas McAllister spent more time congratulating her than he did Arthur and me, and we came in *first* all three times. And Douglas McAllister is the best instructor we have had—ever." She patted Flash on the head. "Arthur said that he was just trying to encourage her. Can you imagine Lisa ever needing any encouragement? She just has a way of making everything she does more special." Madeline stood up. "But you know something, Flash? Arthur doesn't like her much. He called her phony. *Merci! Oui! Mais non!*" Madeline twirled around the kitchen, flipping her hair on top of her head. *"Jamais!"* She slumped back down in the chair. "I'll *never* be like Lisa." Flash put his paws in her lap, raised himself up with effort, and licked her face. "I love you, Flash. You're my best friend. And I'm glad I'm not like Lisa. It's too exhausting." She put her hand gently on Flash's head. "Come on, Flash, let's go to bed," she said, getting up. Flash walked over to his pillow by the bottom of the stairs and lay down. "Oh, all right," Madeline sighed as she bent down and kissed him, "you sleep here tonight. I'll see you in the morning." She felt warm now and sleepy, and, when she went back upstairs to bed, she fell asleep right away.

"Maybe I shouldn't go tonight," Madeline said to her mother the next morning. "Flash doesn't look too well." She was alarmed.

"He's just tired, Mad. You told me you kept him up last night talking. Aunt Ede and I will be here tonight. We'll watch him. Don't worry."

Flash hobbled into the kitchen.

"See what I mean, Mom. He didn't even *want* to come upstairs with me last night. And if something happened to him tonight, I'd never forgive myself." She glanced up and out the window and her voice grew pensive. "Like that night with Dad—"

"Madeline, Flash is all right. It's not the same thing."

"You know, Mom, when Flash and I went out sailing that day, about a week ago—the day I told you about, when he acted the way he always used to—we sailed out really far, farther than I meant to, and it was so strange, there was this big swan out there. Can you believe it—way out in the middle of the Sound? He was all by himself, like he didn't belong to the rest of the swans." Madeline's voice took on a remote tone. "I almost thought I recognized him."

"A swan is a swan," her mother replied matter-of-factly. "The best thing to do is head in the opposite direction."

"That's exactly what we did. We turned around."

"Well, as long as he stays way out there and doesn't bother you, we won't worry about him," her mother said with a smile.

The Commodore's Dance was indeed the event of the summer. Madeline had seen the enormous blue-and-white striped tent before many times. Every Memorial Day, when the Yacht Club officially opened for the season, the tent was raised on the "green," next to the Senior Clubhouse. And every Labor Day, when the Yacht Club closed for the season, the tent appeared again. In between, the two special dates for its presence were the Fourth of July and the Commodore's Dance. Madeline had always attended all the official functions with her father, when all the officers of the Yacht Club stood at attention in their navy-blue blazers with brass buttons and their yachting caps dusted off and covered with gold braid. It was a very serious occasion. But not the Commodore's Dance. Not tonight.

Tonight the tent was filled with Japanese lanterns, glowing all around the top, with a large silver ball rotating in the center, tossing out sparkling lights at the tables and setting the band in motion. The music was even more amplified, as it bounced back and forth against the hulls in the harbor. All of the large yachts had raised flags along their forestays, and several of them had strung Christmas lights around their decks. And the silver sparkles danced on the water while the people danced in the tent.

"What do you suppose the boats talk about when they sit there day after day, rocking back and forth?" Madeline asked Arthur, as they walked down to the dock. Everything was so peaceful now that the band had taken a break and the music had stopped. It was so still. Slowly, Madeline walked out to the far end of the longest dock, peering intently between the seesawing masts. There was something near the mouth of the harbor, in the direction of the summer house, something there in the water, tall and white, caught in moonbeams. She was puzzled. It didn't look like a boat. But, as she rounded the hull of the last boat, for a clear view, the something had vanished.

"I suppose they talk about where they've been," Arthur answered, coming up behind her.

"Huh?" Madeline had forgotten that she had asked Arthur a question.

"The boats, I mean, when they all get together here, for a good rock."

She and Arthur turned around and started

walking back. "Wouldn't it be fun if we could hear them," Madeline pretended. "Maine. Bermuda. Block Island. Newport."

"And *Wild Hunter* over there, she sailed to England," Arthur added.

For a moment, Madeline grew pensive and sad. "*The Great Lady* never even made it to Sunken Island."

"Where's that?"

"Oh, it's a place in the Sound, not too far from here. My father knew about it. He was going— I mean, we were going there, last year, the day he died."

"I never heard of it."

"It was sort of a place he always talked about, like the seven seas, only I guess it's really there."

"No kidding." Arthur seemed interested. "Maybe we should try to find it some day." He took Madeline's hand. "It might be fun."

Madeline shivered slightly. She didn't know if it was a reaction to what Arthur had done or to what he had said.

When she woke up the next morning after a glorious night's sleep, it was a beautiful sunny, clear day. She ate her breakfast quickly and then ran down to the beach for a swim, passing Flash on the way.

"Come on, Flash, help me find some shells. I will make you a necklace!"

"Mad!" she heard her mother call from the house. "Could you help me hang some curtains in your room? It won't take long."

"Okay, coming," Madeline called. "Stay, Flash, I'll be right back."

Flash looked up and wagged his tail slowly.

"Here, watch all my shells for me." She hurried to the house to help her mother.

"Just put the curtains over by the window, and I'll be right up to hang them," Madeline's mother said. "Wait for me! You can hold the ladder. What were you doing down on the beach anyway?"

Madeline had reached the top of the stairs.

"Oh, nothing much. Just picking out a few shells that looked okay for jewelry."

"Not many swans today. Just that one seems to keep swimming back and forth—the big one. I haven't noticed any that big before."

Madeline ran to the window. She remembered last week.

"I'm glad it's high tide, Mad," her mother went on. "I wouldn't want that big one walking around on the beach. Looks like he's the only one out today. You know, Mad, I think that's the one I started painting a few weeks ago. He's come back. Where do you suppose he's been?"

Madeline jerked open the window.

"Mad, are you up there? How do you think the curtains will look?"

Madeline was leaning out the window. The curtains lay crumpled on the floor at her feet. She was staring down at the beach, where she had left Flash. He wasn't there. Instead, she saw his head bobbing up and down in the water, and his tail, like a pendulum, swinging back and forth to the rhythm of the waves. He was swimming straight out toward Long Island in a deliberate course. And then she saw why. He was chasing the swan.

"Flash!" she screamed helplessly from the window.

Then she turned and almost fell over her mother down the stairs.

"Flash, come back! The swan will kill you!"

She ran out the door, down the lawn and hurdled the sea wall in one dash. Then, on the beach, she felt even more helpless.

"Flash, come. Come," she commanded. "Come back, Flash!"

But the dog kept a steady pace behind the swan, not too close. Every few seconds the swan would turn its long neck around and look at the dog.

Flash was out too far now. He had gone way past the float and would never be able to get back to shore, even if he turned around and started back this minute.

"We'll get the boat, Mad! We'll go after him," her mother said, reaching her side. "We'll get him to turn around." They ran to Aunt Ede's dock and clambered aboard *The Lady*. Then, in a mechanical motion, Madeline hoisted the sail, cast off the line, and thrust the boat clear. Her mother quickly settled in the bow. The wind was gusty, and if she could get on the right tack, they could reach the dog shortly. But Madeline wasn't sure what they should do when they did reach him.

Still moving straight ahead, Flash seemed to be gaining on the swan, who was turning around more often now, almost as if it were calling to the dog to hurry and waiting for him to come, urging him on. And the dog responded easily through the tumbling waves. He and the swan were almost together now.

Madeline and her mother were not making much progress. The wind had died down, and the sailboat seemed to inch along backward with the current. Madeline lowered her head and started to cry.

"Look, Mad," her mother called out all of sudden. "Look! The swan! It's bringing Flash back! They've turned around! Look, Mad! Look, way over there, out by the buoy! Look at them! They're coming back!"

The swan had indeed turned around, with Flash following very close behind. They were heading straight for the boat. The swan was leading Flash back! They moved swiftly and were side by side now. Madeline watched and thought she had never seen anything more beautiful: the swan, its long neck rising tall in the water, helping him, bringing back the dog whose head and tail bobbed just above the surface.

Just as Flash reached the boat, Madeline lowered a life ring over the side and grabbed his collar.

The sail went slack in the dead wind as her mother leaned backward to balance the boat. Carefully Madeline worked her hand under the dog's body, still holding the collar tightly with her other hand. With an effort she managed to pull him on board, and he collapsed on the deck.

"Poor Flash. Lie still, lie still."

Madeline's mother picked up the mainsheet from the bottom of the boat and jiggled it. Suddenly, with a jerk, the boat lurched ahead. Madeline hugged the dog tighter, telling her mother what to do at the same time. Her mother pulled the sheet in and the sail filled. In a moment they were home.

Only then did Madeline remember what had happened. She looked back, but the swan was gone.

"How do you like that," her mother said. "Flash has more energy than the two of us put together."

Madeline wondered. "I don't understand him lately. Sometimes he's all worn out and acts so old, yet—"

"I guess sometimes he just feels determined, like you and I do. I remember when your father and I bought Flash, shortly after we were married, your father picked him out because he seemed like a real person."

"But, for a person—" Madeline calculated. "Mom, do you realize that Flash is one-hundred-and-twelve years old!"

Her mother shook her head and smiled. "That's a ripe old age to swim that far—even after a swan."

"Unless the swan is very special," agreed Madeline.

THE SQUALL

JULY always ends on an expectant note. The summer is two-thirds over, and only August remains for completing the memories that have to last all winter long.

Aunt Ede had gone out of town for a few days to a convention, so Lisa had come over to the summer house to stay. Madeline could hardly wait until Aunt Ede came back and Lisa went home. Lisa was endlessly propped in front of a mirror, either giving herself a facial in the bathroom or stretching in and out of outfits in the bedroom. It was surprising that she didn't have arthritis after all that twisting and contorting herself around.

"Has Arthur ever kissed you?" she asked

(129)

Madeline one night as she wiggled into a striped knit dress. She was going out again with Douglas McAllister. Madeline wondered why he hadn't grown tired of her by now. Arthur would have. "Well?" continued Lisa, impatient with the pause.

"No," Madeline stammered. Her face turned scarlet. "Anyway, it's none of your business." She felt an urgent need to change the subject. "When is Charles coming home?"

"*Je ne sais pas!* He never writes to me. You and Aunt Ede get the letters." She tossed Madeline's white sweater over her shoulders. "*Merci!*"

"Don't mention it," Madeline grunted. At least she had turned Lisa's interest from the subject of Arthur. Madeline was not interested in Lisa's next installment of Advice to the Adolescent. Lisa was barely an adolescent herself, and, anyway, she was all talk and no action. That alone was probably the only thing that made her bearable at all. "What do you think, Flash?" Flash shook his head. "So do I. Bor-*innng.*"

"Have fun, Lisa!" she heard her mother call from the kitchen. She picked up some clothes that Lisa had left on the chair. "If I have to share my room with her one more day, I'll— Please, please, Aunt Ede, won't you please come home?" Flash wagged his tail in agreement.

"Madeline," her mother called, "how about supper on the beach, or are you going out?"

"No, Mom. That would be fun! Arthur's busy with his boat for a couple of days."

"Well, why don't I fix something, and we'll eat 'out' tonight. Flash included."

"I'll be right down to help," Madeline answered.

The sky had faded to evening pastels, and the bold afternoon clouds, once piled high across a vivid expanse, were now fragile wisps, yielding to night.

Madeline and her mother spread a checkered tablecloth on the sea wall, and her mother opened the picnic basket.

"This will be fun," her mother said. "It's a perfect night—high tide and an offshore breeze." She set their places and poured some ice tea. "That means no smell—and no bugs."

"Mom, I'm proud of you," Madeline laughed. "You're sounding like a sailor!" Her mother sat down on the sea wall. Madeline thought she looked very tired—It's having Lisa over here all the time, Madeline decided. The water nudged the sand. "Let's take a walk before dinner," she suggested, "that is, if you're not too tired." Her mother slid down onto the sand. "You know, Mom, we lose more and more beach each year." Madeline stood up on the wall and jumped into an approaching wavelet. "I never used to be able to reach the water before at high tide. Something should be done to save our beaches, before they all drown in the sea."

They walked in silence, her mother nearer the sea wall. She guessed her mother, even after all this time, still disliked the touch of salt water. Madeline, on the other hand, couldn't get enough of it, and she squished her toes up and down and around in the cool, mushy sand. It felt wonderful! She could hear Flash's repeated coaxing as he followed along behind the wall; every now and then, his head appeared to remind them. "You *cannot* come down here at high tide any more. There isn't room," she told him. In the distance, the sun slid into the water. For an instant, they saw how very black a summer night can be, until all the tiny lights are turned on by the moon.

Finally, her mother spoke: "Let's make a wish on the evening star."

"Okay, Mom. I wish—"

"Oh, no. You can't say it out loud, or it won't come true," her mother reminded her. They both stopped and stared upward. There were so many things Madeline could wish for: Aunt Ede to come back so Lisa would leave, Charles to come home from his trip so she could tell him what fun times he had missed, Arthur to like her as much as she liked him, and, most of all, that Flash would be all right. Last summer he was. I wish it were last summer, she said to herself. But, all too quickly, she changed her mind. If it were last summer, she wouldn't know Arthur this well, and she wouldn't have been to the Commodore's Dance, and she would still be afraid to go anywhere without Charles, and she wouldn't know her mother as well, and her father—. Oh—I don't know what I wish, she finally decided.

"Madeline," her mother's hand felt cold on her arm, "a while back, when you were talking to me one night about your father, you told me he loved you just the way you were."

Madeline stiffened at the mention of that night. "I didn't mean any of those things I said. I told you that, Mom."

"I know." Her mother's voice picked up. "But you were right. Your father *did* love you just the way you were. And you know something, Madeline," she hurried on, "your father would have loved you even more the way you are now."

Madeline stopped, surprised. "What do you mean?"

"I mean the way you're facing the summer and the way you're figuring it all out for yourself—how to be happy again."

Madeline smiled. "I guess I am happy, Mom." She didn't want her mother moving into a discussion of Arthur, the obvious next step. "Mom, could I ask you something I've wondered about for a long time?"

"Of course, Mad."

Shyly, she touched her mother's hand. "Will you

get married again? I mean to Roger at the gallery or to Laurence, Dad's publisher?"

"I don't think so," her mother answered gently. "They are good friends who neither one would want to follow your father, I'm sure."

Madeline kissed her mother's cheek. "I love you, Mom. I love you as much as I loved Dad." She turned abruptly and ran further down the beach, relishing the cool sand squishing through her toes. Finally she stopped and glanced up at the evening star. "I know what I wish for now," she whispered. "I wish for Mom to be as happy as I am right now."

Later that night she went downstairs and sat in her father's study. Flash pushed the door open with his nose and joined her. The room felt cold, and she welcomed his furry head in her lap. Most of the books were gone, and in their place her mother had displayed his sailing trophies and several pictures of him smiling and holding silver cups. He was so handsome! The bookcase on the other side of the fireplace was filled with his published books. Madeline counted them methodically—nineteen volumes, the result of a lifetime of work. She reached for the last book on the end of the shelf, the one he had finished a year ago. She opened it again to the dedication. She had read it many times before, and she loved the way it sounded: "To my wife who knows, and to my daughter who will find out."

"It sounds great, Dad. What does it mean?" she had asked him.

He had laughed. "I spent more time wording that dedication than I did writing the whole book." He had hugged her. "Think about it long enough and you'll figure it out."

Tears came to her eyes. "You know, Flash, I believe I will." She felt sleepy as she placed the book back on the shelf. "See you tomorrow," she said, as she kissed Flash on the nose. Flash limped back to the kitchen and she heard the thud as he sank into his pillow.

Aunt Ede arrived the next morning in a flurry of excitement. "We got a citation at the convention. Best little newspaper going," she shouted, as she drove through the gate, honking the horn.

"Fantastic!" Madeline's mother flew around the corner of the house. She had been painting at her easel down by the sea wall. "It's lunchtime, Edith, and I'm treating. Come on, Madeline, we'll take Aunt Ede to lunch. I'll run upstairs and change!" Madeline saw that her mother was just as excited as Aunt Ede over the news. That's a great way to be, she thought.

"I'm really happy for you, Aunt Ede," Madeline said earnestly. "It's just great! You're going to end up the biggest newspaper in the state."

"Where's Lisa?"

"At the Yacht Club. Lisa is *very* interested in

sailing this summer—or rather, in getting ready to sail." Aunt Ede laughed. "She's helping the instructor sand the bottoms of some boats."

"Good for her," Aunt Ede said. "A little work won't hurt her."

"I bet she's doing it in gloves," Madeline mused. "Aunt Ede, would you mind too much if I didn't join you for lunch?"

"Of course not. What are *you* up to?"

"I want to finish up *The Lady*. Arthur helped me with the bottom before he left to work on *The Admiral* and I told him I'd clean up the deck and the rails. I've been at it all morning. She's a *big* boat."

Her mother appeared on the stairway. "Coming, Madeline?"

"I'd better not. Aunt Ede said she'd excuse me. Arthur will be over tomorrow, and I'd better finish." She hurried back to the dock. "If you pass the ice cream shop, will you bring me a milk shake!"

She had finished the boat before her mother and Aunt Ede returned. The fiber glass was spotless, and the wood rail was varnished to a high gloss. "Satisfaction!" she beamed. Her father had impressed on her the fine art of keeping a boat shipshape. He would surely have approved of her job today! "Flash!" she called. "Come on! Let's go sailing!" She lay out the sponges on the dock to dry. "Come on, Flash!"

Flash was nowhere in sight, so she headed for the summer house. Her mother's easel was still set up beside the sea wall. Madeline walked over to look at the painting. "Very good," she nodded. "But something's wrong. It's off-balance somehow." She stepped back and studied it for a moment. "I know. It needs a sailboat off to the left—kind of in the distance—a tiny bit of white there to balance the swan. That should do it." She tilted her head. "Yes. Then it would be exactly right." She felt a cold smoosh on her arm. "Hey, I was calling you! Where have you been? Come on! We're going sailing!" and she coaxed Flash along to Aunt Ede's dock.

Cloud upon cloud was piled high across a vivid blue sky, and a brilliant sun shone on the water. Madeline climbed aboard the boat, taking care not to mar the shine. She readied the sails as the water lapped gently against the hull with a steady, lulling sound. Just enough wind promised a perfect afternoon outing. When everything was in readiness, she helped Flash on board. She noticed that a flock of swans had gathered a distance away, rocking aimlessly in the water. "We are going for the best sail we've ever had," she whispered in Flash's ear. "I know, we'll sail to Sunken Island. How would you like that?" She hugged him tight, and he licked her face lovingly.

Madeline pushed the bow away from the dock, hopping over Flash as she seated herself near the tiller. She put the mainsheet between her teeth and pulled in on the line. The sail half-filled, and as she pointed the boat, they caught full sail and were gone. "It's an easterly wind," Madeline told Flash. "Not really too great, but good enough for us." She cleated the mainsheet and the boat surged forward, leaving the swans behind, all except for one who followed for a while.

Straight ahead, far out, she could see a host of large boats. She recognized them as the Atlantics, racing from a yacht club farther down the Sound. There must have been eight or ten of them out there. Madeline had sailed with her father on an Atlantic once. She didn't like them too much. Everyone who sailed them perspired and frowned all the time. It was no fun.

Aside from the Atlantic fleet, she and Flash were the only boat out. Strange, Madeline thought, and it's such a gorgeous day. But at the end of July people usually went away for a few weeks of vacation, and this was the time to sail the Sound as if it belonged to only you.

August had always been her father's favorite month. "If you're in the city, everybody's gone to the country, and if you're in the country, everybody's gone to the mountains," he always had said. "Avoid the mountains, and you have it made." A lifetime of figuring out the month of August—his favorite month—and August was the month he died. That wasn't fair, Madeline thought, that wasn't fair at all.

Dropping her hand over the side, she cupped some water to cool Flash's head. It was then that Madeline noticed the surface of the water. It was transparent, without a ripple, and, ahead of them, a vague line of fog was slowly developing. She had difficulty seeing the Atlantic fleet now, and they seemed to be moving swiftly, farther and farther away. Suddenly, she felt quite uneasy. The compass, mounted above the cabin doors, was steady to the south. She must come about and head north. Many times she had sailed with her father in the middle of infinite water, where a compass was the only guide. But Madeline had always suspected that her father really had a sixth sense about the sea, and, with or without a compass, he would know where they were and where they should go. "Get the feel of the water," he had told her, "and the water will tell you what to do." Madeline could feel the water now, noiseless beneath her, and the feel was unfriendly—too suddenly calm.

"Flash, get ready to come about!" That was the first thing she must do. She must head back to shore. She pushed the tiller, but the boat balked. She tried again but this time the tiller seemed riveted as if it were caught in cement. She could not come about. The sail was luffing and acting weird. All at once the wind began oscillating and shifting and gusting, and she couldn't make out by the telltale feather what was actually happening. But she *did* know that she and Flash were in trouble. And she did know it might be a squall. She had ridden through many squalls with her father, and once with Charles and Tory on the Blue Jay, but this time it was different. It wasn't funny now—there was no one to laugh with. She was in command, and she was responsible for Flash. And she wasn't sure she knew what to do. "Keep down, Flash!" she said, and she quickly put on her life jacket. She should have had it on before. She knew that.

"I must drop sails," she continued, looking upward. There she saw the mackerel sky and the clouds beginning to bank and grow larger and darker to the northwest. She recognized the huge roll cloud forming quickly in the west, with the anvil top, hovering like a great tower, over it. "I don't want to drop sails," she cried loudly. "I want to move! I want to get home!" But she didn't know what the direction was now. The compass needle twitched crazily. There was no way she could head north and hold her course.

Mist was crawling across the water, enveloping her on all sides. And, the entire time, the telltale feather was spinning around like the compass—two hideous tops. The glassy water surface was starting to shudder, and the wind was starting to hum.

She found herself broadside to the chop of waves

that were quickly forming foamy white crests. She knew it was time to drop the mainsail, but she was afraid to stand up. The boat was rocking erratically. Flash lay completely still, as her father had taught him to do. Then, as the wind grew in intensity, the feather steadied. At least now she could tell what she was up against. Now she knew that it was a squall.

She gripped the tiller and managed to push it so they were headed off-wind. It took all her strength to hold the boat on that course so as to prevent an accidental jibe. The bow plunged and rose, and water gushed in at regular intervals. Flash lay perfectly still.

"He trusts me," Madeline said softly, "and I'm not sure if I'll make it."

Then came the line of rain, rushing toward them across the water, with cold, clammy gusts pushing it on. She managed to drop the jib by crawling along the bottom, close to Flash. There was water splashing all over Flash, as the level of water inside the boat grew more alarming. When she released the mainsheet, it billowed and cracked and threw the boom with such great force that Madeline was afraid the mast would break.

All at once she heard the wind scream. The rain turned to hail, and darkness filled the sky. A sudden flash of lightning stabbed the water like an accusing finger, followed by the deep reprimand of thunder!

"Help!" Madeline called out in fright. "Dad, Dad, please help us!" she screamed, as the boat threw her overboard. The words gurgled into the cold, heaving abyss.

"The most important thing to remember if you fall overboard is to swim back to the boat and stay there. Hang on to the side of the boat and wait." Madeline was amazed at the calmness which filled her as she came back to the surface. Those were her father's words. He had always told her to do that in case of an accident.

Then, suddenly, panic struck! "Flash! Flash!" she screamed. Her mouth filled with brine, which stung her lips.

"If someone is sailing with you, and the two of you are thrown overboard, find the other person and never lose sight of him. If he is unable to swim to the boat, find a line and loop it under his arms so you can tow him toward you to the boat." Madeline saw Flash's head, bobbing up and down to the left of her. Stretching an arm over the bow rail, she tried to pull herself up high enough out of the water in order to reach inside the boat and grasp the bow line which she knew was there. With relief she found it and watched it uncoil and tumble into the water in front of her. She held on to it tightly. Flash was swimming toward her, and she was able to catch his collar with her free hand and work her arm around his body. Carefully she pulled them both through the churning water back to the side of the boat. And she waited, strangely calm.

A squall does not last very long, she remembered. Maybe only ten or fifteen minutes. She held them tightly to the line, frozen in position. The water felt cold, and her legs felt numb. "We can last that long, Flash. I know we can!"

Slowly, it became less black overhead, and Madeline saw a touch of blue fighting its way into the western sky. The rain sprinkled the water in almost gentle apology. And the clouds began to break up.

"We made it, Flash. It's over."

But she knew that the worse was yet to come. She and Flash must get back into the boat over a high rail. She would go first and lower the ladder. Then she could pull him up and over. She hoped that he wasn't too tired. "Paddle hard for me," she pleaded, as she nudged him clear of the boat, "just for a minute more Flash, swim."

"You can do it," she assured him.

Grabbing the rail with both her hands, she concentrated all her energy into her arms. She pushed up as hard as she could, but it wasn't enough. She fell back into the water, her arms aching. She was too tired; the rail, too high. She felt helpless. If she were this tired, Flash must be exhausted. Above her, she saw the clear blue sky, but, before she could say anything, she heard a faint sputtering sound from behind her. It grew louder, but she didn't have the strength to turn around.

"Madeline!" Arthur called. "Are you all right?"

"Arthur, over here!" Madeline's eyes filled with tears, and she pushed her wet, sticky hair back, away from her face. "Flash needs help first!" she called.

Arthur easily guided *The Admiral* over to them.

"Don't worry," Arthur told her firmly. "I can manage the dog." He idled the motor.

Madeline was ashamed for ever thinking, even to herself, that *The Admiral* was a piece of junk.

When Arthur had Flash safely on board, he putted over to Madeline. "Can you get back on your boat?"

"I don't think so. I tried once. I think I'm too tired."

"Okay, come on." He pulled her up and onto *The Admiral*. Madeline hugged Flash and rubbed his soaking head. Her arms were aching. Flash lay very still. "Poor Flash," Madeline said. "We didn't get to Sunken Island again."

Arthur leaned over the side. "I have a tow line. We'll tow her back. Unless, of course, you would like to sail her some more today." He smiled at Madeline.

"No thanks, " Madeline answered emphatically, "not today." She settled in the bow, huddled next to Flash. "Where did you ever come from?" she asked. "I thought you were working on *The Admiral* today."

"Take a look—she's perfect!"

"But why were you out in *The Admiral*, in the middle of the Sound in all this weather?"

"Well, when I got back home, I called you, and your mother said *The Lady* was gone, and she heard there might be a squall, and she sounded so upset and—" Arthur reached over and squeezed her hand. "I just thought maybe you might need us."

Before Madeline knew what was happening, Arthur leaned down and kissed her lightly on the mouth. It felt sweet against her parched lips, and she instinctively pressed her arms around him, oblivious to their aching.

The next moment, he sat up again, adjusting the speed of the motor and moving *The Admiral* next to *The Lady*. "I'll fix the rudder so we can tow her," he said, stretching over the side to *The Lady* and locking her rudder in place. "Make sure she stays in line back there. Keep an eye on her for me." He finished and sat back in *The Admiral*, speeding up the motor. "Now, let's get home."

Madeline's head was spinning, and her legs felt spongy as she settled on the center seat, facing Arthur. She looked at him, she looked at her boat, and, beyond her boat, she caught sight of a faint white apparition, floating tall in the gentle waves.

August

REGATTA TIME

EVERY year, during the second week in August, the Yacht Club sponsored a two-day racing event called The Blue Jay Regatta. A hundred and twenty Blue Jay–class boats crowded into the harbor and emptied over two hundred visiting children and teenagers into the village. The fourteen-foot sailboats and their crews came from invited yacht clubs along the Sound, and the regatta was the high point of the Junior sailing season.

Last year, Madeline and Charles had come in first in one of the races for their division, but they had ended up sixth overall in all four divisions. The divisions were organized according to the last number that appeared in large black numerals on the mainsail of each boat. Madeline's sail number was 4789, and she and Charles had realized three years ago that the *9* division had, just by chance, the fastest, most experienced boats in the regatta.

"That's good," her father had said. "You'll be up against the best—a real challenge!"

"In other words, hard. Yuck." Madeline had wished she could jumble up the numbers and come out with 4 at the end. The *4* division always seemed to be the beginners. Anyway, after some good luck, plus expertise on her part and Charles's last year, they had done *almost* all right.

"Not bad," her father had remarked proudly, "sixth out of a hundred and twenty boats!"

However, Madeline had been bitterly disappointed. They had missed being first overall by just a few points. If only she had not misjudged that mark in the first race, and if only Charles had not tangled the spinnaker in the second race, and if only the wind had not died on the second day— If only, if only, if only . . .

" 'If onlys' are poor excuses," her father had said. "They're a waste of good thinking time. Think ahead!" he had told her. "Say *next* time!' "
Sometimes Madeline had been puzzled by her father. For a student of history, looking ahead seemed out of character. Unless, she had finally decided, by looking ahead he could better understand the past. *Next* time, she had determined,

I'll win first place overall in the regatta, and our yacht club will have the silver trophy at last.

Now *next* time was here. "There's a lot of hard work coming up," she told Flash, as she was getting dressed for sailing class the morning before the regatta. Flash pricked up his ears, but his head did not move. If only he were not so tired and feeble . . . Madeline pulled her hair into a ponytail and swished it over her shoulder. It was nearly as long as Lisa's now. It almost reached her waist. She patted Flash on the nose. "*Next* time you will not be tired and feeble. And, *next* time," she said, thinking back to the day of the squall, shuddering slightly, "we'll get to Sunken Island."

The class day was spent readying the boats for racing and preparing the markers to set the race courses. Huge styrofoam cones were hauled out from the storage space under the Junior Clubhouse. Repainted a glistening white, they stood like miniature hills of snow caught in the sunlight across the parking lot. On the top of each one was planted a long pole with a brightly colored toeless sock dangling from its peak. The sock was appropriately called a "windsock," and out on the water it was not only decorative but also informative. Each mark had its own individual sock color, and, as the wind filled the sock, the sailor could tell the correct course for the race as well as the wind's direction as he approached each mark.

Arthur and Madeline spent the whole day getting the marks ready. Arthur believed in sanding the bottom of a boat and slicking it down right before the race to make her fast, so he and Madeline would tend to *Banana Peel* in the morning.

Douglas McAllister and Lisa left late in the afternoon with five meticulous marks aboard the committee boat. They would set them down at designated points somewhere out on the Sound, and the next morning the race courses would be determined according to the type of day it was.

"Tomorrow morning," Arthur told her, as they stood on the dock, watching the committee boat leave the harbor, "we'd better be here at the club, ready to work, by seven. The bottom of that boat has to be extra slick and fast."

Madeline winced. "So early?" But seeing Arthur's frown, she said, "Aye, aye, sir. See you at seven."

Madeline's alarm rang unmercifully. Hazy light illuminated the curtains, giving her room a soft glow. The weather was going to be good. By midmorning, a breeze would push in and blow away the fog. August days always started out like this. When she opened the bedroom door, Flash was waiting.

"Good morning, sir," Madeline addressed him. "What are you doing upstairs?"

Flash answered by coaxing her down the hall.

Then he walked over to the window at the top of
the stairs and stood with his front paws on the sill.
Madeline followed him and looked out. There was
a flock of swans gliding by the beach, about twelve
of them.

"Oh, no you don't, not today. No playmates. I'm
not going to be home. You cannot have friends over
when I'm not home. You know that," Madeline
whispered, listening to see if her mother was
moving about downstairs. All was silent, and
Madeline gently pulled Flash down from the
windowsill. "Come on, be a good boy. We'll go
downstairs and fix your breakfast." Flash limped
slowly down and headed straight for the front door.
"All right, sir, I'll trust you. But leave the swans
alone," and she opened the door. In a few minutes,
he was back. Madeline was pleasantly surprised. A
dozen swans may have been tempting, but he was
an obedient child. "Good Flash!" Madeline said as
she gave him some biscuits. "See you later. I have
to get ready."

Madeline pedaled her bicycle briskly toward the
Yacht Club, stopping for a few minutes by the town
green. The dampness of early morning could hardly
dull the picture. The harbor was crowded with small
boats of every color. They looked like the tiny
wooden boats she used to lay out on a bright-blue
handkerchief when she was a little girl. She called

it her harbor scene, and she would spend hours moving each little piece back and forth and in and out. Sometimes her creation would get so crowded that the boats would run into each other. She hoped that wouldn't happen today when a hundred and twenty Blue Jays set sail for the open Sound. Quickly she climbed back on her bicycle and rounded the corner into the parking lot.

"We even beat the launchmen this morning," Arthur announced with obvious pleasure. He had pulled *Banana Peel* on her trailer to a space beside the hoist and was already scrubbing the bottom of the boat. "I just checked the sign-up sheet before you came," he went on. "It looks as if we're up against twenty boats so far in our division. I think there are a few new ones."

"I hope they're not as good as the old ones," Madeline said.

"Scrub hard," Arthur told her. "If we don't get her into the water by eight, we'll have to wait our turn at the hoist. Then we're sure to lose that mooring at the mouth of the harbor."

Madeline remembered explaining to Flash once the difference between *Banana Peel* and *The Lady,* and why she never took him sailing in the Blue Jay. Blue Jays are called "dry sailors," and, except for Regatta-times, they are never left in the water unless their sails are full. Otherwise, they sit stoically on their trailers in the club parking lot, sails furled, glancing down enviously upon their floating counterparts. "It's easier for you just to step aboard *The Lady* at Aunt Ede's dock," Madeline told Flash. Flash wagged his tail in understanding. It was all right with him. Anyway, he didn't go down to the Yacht Club any more.

Arthur pushed ahead on the waxing as Madeline polished hard, her knuckles turning chalk-white. She knew it was much easier to sail out of the harbor, tacking around stationary boats. If they waited too long, it would be a mob scene.

By nine, Madeline and Arthur had secured *Banana Peel* at the choice mooring at the mouth of the harbor, and they were back again to help other boats into the water. When the last boat was down at ten, Madeline and Arthur took the launch out to her boat. She and Arthur climbed aboard and went right to work with the rigging and the sails.

"We have plenty of time," Arthur judged. "The committee boat hasn't even left the dock."

"Dad always said not to rush. Give yourself plenty of time. Be at the starting line before anybody else. Know your course. Know your markers. Study the wind out there. Feel the current. Be sure of the tide." Madeline recited the remembered instructions, as if she were ticking off a list.

"Yes, ma'am," Arthur said.

When Madeline raised the sail, the boom moved

and a swan became visible. It was no more than ten feet away. Madeline hoisted the mainsail and pulled herself toward the jib, where she could see it more clearly. The swan was enormous, with long smooth feathers puffing out its back. Its head dipped leisurely in and out of the water, and the pastel-orange beak softly pressed the ripples. It didn't look frightening or strange or unpredictable. It didn't look like the rest of the swans. It didn't look mysterious. Maybe that was because it didn't wear a mask.

"Look at the swan!" Madeline called to Arthur, who was checking the rudder for her. "We can't hit him!" She hoped the swan wouldn't follow the boat. She remembered one time it had.

"I see him!" Arthur called, as he hauled the mainsheet in. A gust of wind from the open Sound caught the sail. "Ignore the bird! He's not interested in us!" And Madeline decided, with relief, that Arthur was right. The swan did not follow the boat.

Sailing close in to shore past Madeline's house, they could see her mother standing on the sea wall. Madeline and Arthur waved, and her mother lowered the binoculars and waved back. Then Madeline pointed the boat outward, and they headed for the committee boat. The last thing Madeline saw was Flash walking slowly along the beach, and the swan floating toward him, against the shoreline.

"Trim the mainsheet and let her heel!" Madeline

called, as the boat tipped hard to one side. She relished the freedom of the wind.

Arthur put the mainsheet in his teeth and leaned way out over the rail. He's as strong as Charles, Madeline thought, watching him with admiration.

But the exhilaration of the sail was quickly dispelled, as always, when they reached the starting line, that invisible line between the bow of the committee boat and a designated buoy. Twenty-five boats clustered around the committee boat at various angles, in various states of noise and confusion, like people gathering around an entrance, jostling one another for position. As many times as Madeline had raced, she had never gotten used to starting lines. She guessed that the boats didn't like starting lines either, and that's why they acted so erratically. Starting lines held them back and forced them to act against their nature. Madeline glanced at the faces inside the boats. They were nearly all familiar faces, ones she had seen year after year, each year growing a little older-looking, with a few slight wrinkles emerging along their foreheads, probably from too many textbooks in the winter and too many races in the summer. Eyes darted back and forth, checking everyone's equipment from the tops of the masts to the rudder pins. Stopwatches were punched on and off, and booms swung in crazy designs.

Madeline tacked back and forth along the starting line, holding the boat as near center as she was able, checking her own stopwatch at regular intervals. Her father's words rang through her head: "Be the first to cross the line! Then you'll have clear air!" Madeline knew how important clear air was. If one or two other sails got in your way and you had to share some wind, then your mainsail would be robbed of the full force and momentum of full free air.

The buzzer sounded the five-minute warning. "We're in good shape!" Arthur said. "Enough time to relax!"

"Relax!" Madeline gasped. "I could scream!"

There was the two minute warning. Startled at the sharp sound, Madeline remembered her father taking her to the museum one afternoon. He was doing research on his last ancient history book. They were in the Greek exhibit when the warning bell sounded for the museum closing. Her father was finishing up some notes. By the time they had reached the front door, it was locked. One hour went by before the night watchman found them. Her father had laughed. "This is heaven for me! Imagine being surrounded by everything I love the most!" But Madeline hadn't thought it was heaven. It was spooky, and she had wished they'd heeded the warning signal.

When the ten-second buzzer sounded, Madeline and Arthur were exactly ten seconds from the starting line. Madeline had counted it off in her mind, and she was right on target. But as the gun went off, a boat suddenly veered in front of them from their port side.

"Protest!" Arthur shouted, as they crossed the line, pushed off to an angle. She fended off the intruder, shouting "Protest!" again. The word "Protest" filled the air, and pandemonium set in. Arthur sat in dead-center of the boat, scrunched down, his eyes darting back and forth, checking all directions at once. Madeline gritted her teeth and forged ahead. Finally, they took the wind and sailed free, leaving a floundering stew of boats behind. They were on a lifted tack, the wind having suddenly shifted, propelling them directly toward the first mark. The bright-green windsock was pointing them around.

"Ready about!" Madeline called, stretching her neck down and forward as she peered through the small plastic window in the sail. Arthur moved quickly, and they swung around the first mark at least four boat-lengths ahead of everyone else.

Arthur looked up at the telltale feather. "We're lucky with the wind today. Two more marks, and we've won the race!"

As they approached the second mark, its bright-yellow windsock bobbed erratically, making the wind direction more difficult to determine. Madeline came up on the second mark a little close.

"Watch it, Madeline," Arthur snapped, as he pinched the sail. With great relief, Madeline just cleared it, still holding their comfortable lead.

But, the red windsock on the third mark proved to be a poor omen. Madeline tacked too soon, and they missed the mark completely. She had to make an extra tack, turning the boat around and backtracking several boat-lengths in order to correct her mistake, and she and Arthur lost valuable time. They ended up in the middle of competitors. Two boats had rounded the mark ahead of them, and they would have to give way to a third. Arthur was obviously annoyed. She had forfeited their lead, and they no longer had clear air. The most they could possibly hope for now was fourth place. "Damn it all!" she heard Arthur mutter under his breath. Madeline jabbed the tiller in disgust, tears clouding her eyes.

It was then that she saw the swan off in the distance, off the stern, in the wake of the boat. She blinked her eyes hard, thinking she saw something else, swimming beside it, but she couldn't be sure.

Suddenly, she screamed, "Flash!" She dropped the tiller and rushed to the rail. The boat tipped, throwing Arthur off-balance, and he stumbled over the centerboard trunk. As the sail flapped wildly above her, Madeline stood transfixed.

"What are you *doing?*" Arthur pulled himself back onto the rail. He stared at her in disbelief.

Then, in an instant, the swan was gone. All they saw now was a parade of boats passing them and crossing the finish line. They were last!

Madeline sat rigidly, afraid of falling apart. She didn't dare look at Arthur, who, she could feel, was still staring at her. "I'm sorry, Arthur," she began in a small voice, "I'm really sorry." Arthur said nothing. "I'll make it up in the next race."

When Arthur finally spoke, his voice was as cold as a splash of water across her face. "Madeline, you know very well that to come in *dead-last* in *any* race will probably cost us the series."

Stunned, Madeline matched his icy tone. "Not if we come in *dead-first* two times." And nothing more was said.

Banana Peel was moored and unrigged in silence at the mouth of the harbor. Madeline, too, was terribly upset. She had never, in her long record of races, *ever* come in dead-last.

The day had been a disaster, she decided as she rode her bicycle toward home.

"Mom, was Flash home all day?" Madeline asked that evening, out of curiosity.

"I guess so." Her mother put away the last dish from supper. "I was busy painting most of the day. You know that swan I told you about, the one I started painting a few weeks ago? Well, it came back and I finished the picture." She walked into the other room. "Come here a minute and have a look. What do you think?"

Madeline followed her mother and slowly looked

up at the painting, which was propped on top of a bookcase. "It's nice, Mom. But what about Flash?"

"He was around the beach, I guess. Why?"

"Oh, nothing. I just thought I saw him out swimming, that's all."

"I don't think so, Mad. He doesn't seem too well today. He seems pretty tired."

Madeline was studying her mother's painting. "I like it a lot, Mom. Except for one thing. The real swan doesn't wear a mask."

"All swans wear masks," her mother said.

Madeline dropped the subject. "You know, Mom, you're right about Flash being tired," she said, as they walked back into the kitchen. "Look at that. He hasn't eaten a thing."

The next day, Madeline made a definite point of arriving at the mooring before Arthur so she could rig the boat herself and prepare for the day's races. That way she and Arthur could avoid any discussion. He had overreacted yesterday. One bad race shouldn't spoil a friendship. She decided to forgive him.

"He'll think about it overnight, and after he's slept on it things won't seem so bad. He'll be all right," her mother assured her.

But when Arthur arrived on the boat, the same coldness arrived with him. "I hope you don't see any more swans today," he said pointedly, "*and* I hope that stupid, old *dog* of yours is safely locked up in the kitchen."

Madeline looked him straight in the eyes, and she bit down hard on her lower lip. She didn't believe her ears. Stupid dog! Old dog! Flash! How dare he say that! She forced the tiller: "Set sail!" The words sizzled. She was stuck with this pompous jerk for one more day and two more races, but after that he could go off and drown!

Douglas McAllister was assigned to the committee boat for the second day of races. There were two races scheduled, one in the morning and one after lunch. Madeline had planned on having her lunch very near the committee boat so she could talk to Lisa and wouldn't be stuck with the All-American Jerk.

Banana Peel won the first race easily—just as Madeline had vowed she would. They tacked over to the committee boat for lunch.

"Congratulations!" Douglas McAllister called, as Madeline pulled up alongside and threw a line to Lisa. Lisa, in turn, tossed two peanut butter and jelly sandwiches to them and a big bag of grapes. "You were a good thirty seconds ahead of the second boat! If you win this afternoon's race as easily, we stand a very good chance . . ." No one dared finish the sentence.

"We *will* win this afternoon's race," Madeline promised.

"Merveilleux!" exclaimed Lisa in her most passionate French. *"Les champions!"*

By noon, the weather clouded up and the air turned chilly. Madeline hoped, however, for the same steady, brisk wind that had held the boat so easily on course and pushed it victoriously over the finish line that morning. Now she and Arthur were leading the competition in all four divisions by three points. If they won the afternoon race, they would surely win the silver trophy.

Maybe, Madeline thought, just maybe Arthur is sorry about his bad temper. She turned to him, as the other boats began to prepare sails for the race. "Do you want to skipper this afternoon? It's all right with me."

Arthur looked at her, unsmiling. "Why? You did all right today. Why cop out now?"

Madeline stiffened. "Cop out?" She spit out the words harshly. I'll show him how I cop out. The same way I showed my mother. He'd just better stand aside. "Trim the mainsheet *hard,*" she commanded, as they sailed across the starting line with a good, strong lead, "and do just as I say. And I'll show you *exactly* how I cop out!" Anger blurred her eyes, and she couldn't make out for sure if a smile crossed Arthur's face.

It was a hard race. The wind shifted crazily, as if to herald an approaching storm. Madeline's head ached from concentration, and her eyes were stinging from salt spray. She and Arthur had worked like two absolute strangers, respectful and professional, doing a job. They had done the job well. They had won. Now Madeline was glad it was over.

When they arrived back at the dock, Arthur put his arm around her shoulder. "Great." But he said the word too calmly to suit Madeline. She jerked herself free and walked up onto the porch of the Senior Clubhouse, where a large shining cup rested majestically on a table, surrounded by flowers.

To sail the seven seas and to come home a winner! Her father's motto.

Madeline stood trembling on the porch, ready to accept the silver trophy. She was nervous, and she felt so alone. It would have been more comfortable to lose, she thought, to be absorbed in the crowd below. She longed to be down at the hoist with Douglas McAllister and Lisa, helping to raise a hundred boats out of the water. She had an overwhelming desire to fill water balloons and pull boat trailers into the parking lot and find everyone's lost gear and do anything to get down off the porch. The porch had never seemed so high before, like being on a pedestal. And, even though the clouds lay like slabs of gray marble and the air seemed just as cold, Madeline felt hot and sticky.

"I accept this trophy for our club on behalf of

Arthur and myself." She choked slightly on the word "Arthur," but no one seemed to notice. The words tolled like bells against her ears.

"Over here!" Aunt Ede called, above the whistles and applause. She clicked her camera several times.

Madeline noticed Arthur's mother and father on the steps. His mother was holding on to his father's arm—the way people looked in those stiff, old-fashioned portraits.

"Bravo! Bravo!" Lisa shouted as loudly as she could and still remain regal. Suddenly, Madeline remembered Charles. She wondered when he was coming home. He would know what to do about Arthur.

Madeline's mother looked as if she were crying. Her mother had always cried when her father had stood on the porch like this. She said it made her feel so proud and happy!

Madeline wondered why she herself didn't feel happy. She glanced hesitantly over at Arthur who had been pushed up beside her. He looked frozen. Of course, that's what was wrong. It was his fault. He was spoiling their victory. He was so sour and sullen. What had she ever seen in him, anyway? He was too tall, and his bright-red hair, sprouting out all over his head, made him look ridiculous. He reminded her of the Raggedy Andy doll she had had as a little girl—only without the smile. Why had she wasted her summer on him?

Madeline looked down again at the people clustered below—her mother, Aunt Ede, Lisa—her family.

"Oh, Dad, I wish you were here!" she whispered half aloud.

FLASH

"MADELINE," her mother began slowly, "it's really none of my business, but I've been wondering—" She stopped, waiting for some sign from Madeline.

"I know what you want to know, Mom."

"It's just that I was down in the village, and Mr. Robinson had put a picture of you and Arthur up in his window." She added, brightly: "I guess you know the two of you are the village celebrities."

"I don't like Arthur any more," Madeline stated simply, and she told her mother the whole story. "Now what do you think?"

"Well, frankly, Madeline, I think you're the one who's overreacting. I don't think Arthur meant anything by it." Madeline humphed. "You know,

Mad, some men are very stubborn that way. They may know that they've been wrong, but they don't like to apologize."

"Dad was never like that," Madeline said, defensively. "Besides, Arthur isn't even a sailor. So what right has he to make judgments?"

"Well, he evidently is a good enough crew," her mother answered. "And, I think, Madeline, he *did* try to apologize. I think he's really sorry."

"I doubt it. He's stubborn. Even when we were little, Arthur was stubborn. Charles could tell you that."

"Well, now you're being stubborn, too, Mad."

Madeline shrugged. "It's his loss!" she trilled lightly. "Lisa's introducing me to a friend of Douglas McAllister's today. I'm branching out!" She skipped upstairs, stopping by the window. Flash was lying on the beach over by Aunt Ede's dock. "Flash! Flash! Stay where you are!" she called. "I'll be right down, and we'll go sailing!" She could meet Douglas McAllister's friend tomorrow. There was no hurry.

She ran into her room, glancing in the mirror as she passed by. Even though her hair was as long as Lisa's now, she didn't like wearing it down. "Ponytails are babyish," Lisa had told her. "Men like to see hair, not the rear end of a horse." Madeline preferred the rear end of a horse, for loose hair got all snarled and straggly when you sailed.

Her legs were almost as long as Lisa's now, too. She extended them in turn and pointed her toes. The only difference seemed to be one or two scratches, a rope burn on her ankle, and a few black-and-blue marks on one thigh, where the tiller had jabbed her. Sailing scars are hard to hide. "Oh, bother it all—I'll just have to be myself!" she said aloud.

"Madeline!" her mother called up the stairs. "Lisa's here. She's ready to go!"

"Tell her I'll meet her later!" She remembered that Flash was waiting for her on the beach. They were going sailing.

She peered from behind the curtains to make sure Lisa had gone before she ran downstairs to join her dog. The wind was gusting, and the water coughed up white caps. Madeline raced across the lawn and over the sea wall. "It looks like a good sailing day, Flash," Madeline told him, sinking into the sand beside him. He didn't move. "Flash?" Madeline tried to lift him, but his head felt so heavy. "Mom! Come here! Hurry!" Her mother came running from the house. Madeline cradled Flash's head in her arms. She was shaking all over. "He's dead, Mom. I know he's dead. He died alone, like Dad." Her mother dropped to the sand beside her, and finally Flash opened his eyes. Madeline burst into grateful sobs. "Oh, Flash! You scared me so! What's the matter? What's wrong?" Her mother touched Madeline's shoulder and pointed out toward the harbor buoys. Madeline realized for the first time that his coat was soaking wet. "Oh, Flash, you didn't. You went after the swan again." Flash wagged his tail heavily.

"We'll take him up to the house, Mad. He'll be all right."

The tide was coming in fast, covering the dog's feet and legs.

"What if I hadn't remembered him, Mom? *He would have drowned!*"

"Madeline, it's all right. You *did* remember him. He didn't drown."

Madeline helped Flash to his feet. His fur was ice cold. "I love you, Flash," she repeated over and over again as they walked slowly to the house, and she guessed that she loved him more at that moment than she ever had in her entire life. She placed his pillow near the door, and rubbed him briskly with a large towel. He lay down at once and went to sleep.

Charles was coming home the next day. His letter to Aunt Ede said that he would be on the evening plane and to please meet his limousine. He had given up writing to Madeline because, he said, she never answered his letters. Madeline knew that Charles would understand how busy she had been, but she also knew that he would be disgusted by her quarrel with Arthur. Charles had no patience with Flash any more, either. "I can't wait until they both get old, and nobody wants them," she thought as she sat down beside Flash and stroked his head.

"I don't believe it, Mom. The summer went by so fast."

"Yes, it did, but you and Arthur accomplished a lot."

Madeline had been thinking about Arthur quite a bit. Now that the sailing lessons had ended, there wasn't much chance that she would run into him "*accidentellement*," as Lisa would say. Besides, she was embarrassed about the whole thing, and time just made it worse. Lisa had seen him twice in the village, and she reported that he looked very pale and sad.

"I feel terrible about him," Madeline had said to Lisa.

"But you did *nothing, chérie! He* is at fault!"

"I don't care," Madeline had insisted. "I miss Arthur."

"I think I'll sail over to the club and check on *Banana Peel*," Madeline told her mother that day at lunch. "I haven't seen her since the regatta, and she probably needs some attention." Madeline knew that *Banana Peel* was all right. She had taken the boat out of the water herself and placed her back on the trailer in her proper space. "She's probably collected water from the rain," Madeline added. "I'll have to bail her out." She got up quickly from the table and carried her dishes over to the sink. "I'll take Flash with me. He seems okay this afternoon." She nudged Flash from his nap. "Come on. I need some company. And some moral support," she added, as she and Flash walked over to Aunt Ede's dock and climbed aboard *The Lady.* "You know, Flash, I don't think *The Lady* has even met *Banana Peel,* and they're sisters!" The idea made her smile. "I guess *The Lady* met *The Great Lady* once. What a really wonderful family!" She waved to her mother, who was crossing over to Aunt Ede's house. "We'll be back in time for supper!"

The club was nearly deserted when Madeline and Flash arrived. Many large yachts were missing from their moorings—probably on their last long sail of the summer before returning to their winter ports. Madeline moored *The Lady* in one of the empty spaces near the center of the harbor and blew her horn for the launch to take them into the dock.

"He's a beautiful dog," the launchman said, as Flash struggled down the steep launch steps. "How old is he?"

"He's sixteen," Madeline answered proudly.

The launchman leaned over and patted Flash. "I remember him from last year. But you haven't brought him down this year at all."

"He's not much of a sailor now," Madeline said, "but he's good company."

"Your boat's had good company too," the

launchman smiled. "Arthur's been over there, working hard, sprucing her up for several days now."

Madeline brightened. "Really!"

"He's sure proud of her. He said he'd clean her up till she shined!"

He steered the launch up to the dock. "Thank you very much," Madeline said, and she helped Flash onto the dock. The dog hobbled up the ramp and hurried over to greet Arthur, who patted his back and rubbed him vigorously. Well, if Flash isn't mad at Arthur, why should I be? Madeline decided.

Arthur looked up at her. "Truce," he said quietly, giving her a hesitant smile.

Filled with relief, Madeline reached over and impulsively took hold of his hand. "Thank you for taking care of *Banana Peel*. She looks just great!"

"I owed it to both of you," Arthur winked. "And to Flash I owe an apology."

Madeline was trembling. Her mother had underestimated Arthur. He had actually apologized. "Would you like to sail home with me? We're getting things ready for Charles. He's coming home tomorrow."

"Yes, he wrote me."

This time Madeline didn't care that Arthur knew—probably long before she did. She only cared that Arthur knew how grateful she was. "*Mon Dieu!*" she could hear Lisa, in her mind, "*he* is at fault!" Oh shut up, Lisa, she thought crossly.

"I'd like to go home with you," Arthur was saying. "Let me put this stuff away." Madeline helped him gather up the cleaner and sponges. "I'll be back in a minute," he told her.

Madeline looked around. There was still evidence of the regatta, although the many boat trailers that had crowded the village green were gone now. They had left behind only the souvenir of tire tracks in the grass. Bits and pieces of multicolored balloons still stuck to the pavement and the sides of the boats now in dry dock, reminiscent of glorious water fights in the parking lot. Madeline picked up a few stray pieces of wire and line and slipped them into the garbage bin. Streamers and ragged pennants spilled limply over the top. The whole club seemed still worn out from the regatta.

As Madeline waited for Arthur, she walked out on the dock. There she noticed small splashes appearing at random on the surface of the now smooth water. Those would be the bunkers leaping to avoid the blues, another sure sign of summer's end. Madeline was no fisherman, but she was familiar with the notorious bluefish who invaded the Sound in August and drove the other fish wild. Those ugly, big fish hounded the deepest waters, pushing the other fish to the surface and popping them out. Her father had said they were almost as mean as sharks. Poor little bunkers, Madeline thought. They don't stand a chance.

Fascinated, Flash was lying on the end of the

longest dock with his head hanging over the edge. He was tracking the tiny eruptions back and forth with his eyes. His ears twitched, and he wiggled, but he didn't try to catch them now, the way he used to. He wasn't a sailor *or* a fisherman any more, Madeline decided. He was just too tired.

The launch took the three of them back to *The Lady*. Dozens of clouds wisped across the sky like remnants of cotton candy.

"Shall we take her for a perfect sail?" Madeline smiled at Arthur. "This time you can skipper."

Arthur slipped the boat from the mooring. "I'd be most pleased," he said, then seated himself at the tiller. Flash took his place in the stern, near Arthur's feet, and Madeline raised the mainsail.

As they passed the tall reeds around the bend, the swan floated out. Madeline caught sight of him first across the boom angle. The swan rose tall and stately in the high grass, like a commander in charge of his territory.

"Watch out for the swan!" she heard herself call to Arthur. "It's off starboard!"

"Hang on to Flash!" Arthur called back.

"Flash will take care—" Madeline stopped in mid-sentence. All of a sudden she had an eerie feeling. She felt it was all happening again. It was the end of summer. The three of them were in a boat. They were leaving the harbor on a beautiful day for a perfect sail. Then, for no apparent reason, a swan appeared, a strange and different swan, a swan that didn't wear a mask, a huge swan who was always alone.

Madeline felt cold, and she was very frightened. She knew that the swan would follow the boat for a while. She knew that Flash would growl. And then—

"Madeline! Madeline!" Arthur broke her reverie. "Trim the mainsail! This is your captain speaking! Here's the best wind we've had all summer!"

Madeline stiffened until she went numb. Last summer. An August afternoon. At the end of summer. Her father had said those very words! She remembered it vividly even now.

With trembling hands, she yanked hard on the mainsheet and cleated it tight. As the sail filled, the boat surged ahead. Maybe, if they could sail fast enough . . . She was so afraid, and she shuddered.

Flash perked up his ears, and his eyes followed the huge swan, who was following the boat now, as Madeline knew it would. But Flash did not growl. Instead, his tail was wagging in happy circles, and he turned and looked at Madeline with reassurance. Then he dropped his heavy head down in her lap.

The swan rose slowly into the air, and once again the boat grew dark in its shadow.

"Madeline!" Arthur called. "Look at that!"

Madeline's eyes filled with tears, and her throat felt hot and dry. "Don't leave, Flash—not for a while," she whispered. "We have to finish our sail, you know." She buried her face against his ruff. Flash licked her hands gently.

"Ready about!" Arthur announced briskly from the tiller. "We'll head in now!"

"No!" Madeline shouted with urgency. "Not yet! Let's sail for Long Island!"

"But I thought you wanted to get things ready for Charles!"

"Later! There'll be more time later!" And she pulled Flash up on the rail so they could feel the wonderful sea spray against their faces.

THE SWAN

"WHERE are we headed?" Arthur asked. "Would the mate please report to the captain."

Madeline was still clinging to Flash, oblivious to the question.

"Repeat! Repeat! Captain to crew! Captain to crew!" He mimicked a public-address system. "What is our course?"

Slowly Madeline raised her head and took a breath. "Southwest by south! Two hundred and ten degrees!" she answered, smiling at last. "There's an island. Dad and I almost saw it once last year. Let's go there!"

"What island?" Arthur inquired, puzzled. "There's no island near here."

"I didn't say 'near here,' but with this wind, we'll be there in no time."

The wind was steady, out of the northwest, exactly right for their course. It was the kind of wind that comes with the end of summer, steady and strong. Madeline knew that the wind would stay with them. She knew that they would find the island. She knew that the weather would be beautiful, and she knew that they would be home in time for supper. Everything would happen today, just as it had happened a long, long time ago—at the end of last summer. Only this time they would reach the island.

"It is a special island," her father had told her. "It rises right out of the sea like an enchanted kingdom, but only at certain times." Madeline was sure that today would be one of those times.

"Okay, Madeline," Arthur agreed. "I'm in no hurry. I have until tomorrow!"

"Well, it won't take that long," Madeline replied, rather sadly, looking at Flash. "It will just take today," she whispered to him, "and it will be perfect."

Dead ahead, to Arthur's astonishment, an island appeared, just as Madeline had promised. It broke through the water, dwarfing the waves, and its hues were rich and full. Golden rays of sunlight streamed through the clouds and slanted toward its base.

Above its peak, a vivid arch of colors hung, catching the sun and forming a rainbow.

Madeline's eyes were opened wide, and she felt almost suspended in air, floating somewhere in a dense, cool space.

It was Arthur who pulled her back to reality. "Well, I'll be damned," he laughed. "I've been running around Long Island Sound all my life, and I never ran into this one!"

Madeline shook her head with a jerk. "Of course you didn't," she said. "You never looked for it. It's on the chart." She reached down and pulled a chart from a drawer under the seat. "Here! And if you don't veer off, you'll run into it—but good—this time!"

Arthur glanced at the chart as he turned the boat into the wind to check their speed. At the same time, Madeline loosened the mainsheet, and they drifted to a stop.

"I'll be damned!" he repeated. "That's Sunken Island!"

Sunken Island was only a nuisance to real boat people. It was something to be avoided, a pile of rocks dangerously invisible in the middle of Long Island Sound. At high tide, the jagged granite tips just barely broke the surface between waves, sometimes with only swirls of water as telltales. And at low tide, no one had ever bothered to check it out, as far as Arthur knew. It was way beyond the racing courses, and if one day some poor sailor or motorboat *did* run aground on it, he would be too embarrassed to admit it. Only Madeline's father had deliberately sought it out one day.

Flash hurried over to the railing.

"You'll be the first one out, Flash. I promise," Madeline said.

Flash didn't wait. He climbed up with his paws on the rail and jumped into the water with no effort. Madeline watched him in amazement.

"It's a beautiful place, Dad said!" Madeline called to Arthur.

The water was as clear as glass. Madeline couldn't believe how blue and transparent it was. Imagine murky Long Island Sound hiding a pool of Caribbean waters.

"Let's anchor here!" she called to Arthur, who nodded as he stared in amazement at the water.

Madeline released the anchor line and watched it uncoil until the anchor hit bottom. A small cloud of sand erupted to the surface. "It's dead low tide now," Madeline informed Arthur. "It's hardly deep here at all." However, she noted curiously, there wasn't a low-tide smell.

"How long do you think we have?" Arthur asked, glancing at his watch. "I mean, how long before the whole thing sinks again?"

Madeline scratched her head. "Oh, a few hours, I suppose. Then I guess the beach sort of starts to disappear. I'm sure we'll be able to tell." She shook her head. "It's weird, isn't it. But isn't it great!" She shivered slightly as a delicate wisp of air sent tiny wavelets along the boat, settling it comfortably into place. "This is when your philosophy course can come in handy," Madeline smiled.

Arthur was visibly stunned. "It's uncanny, Madeline. You found a secret tropical island right here in the middle of Long Island Sound." He beamed at her. "Madeline, you're terrific!"

"It's a very special place," she added, joining him at the rail. "At least, Dad said it was. Actually, he's the one who found it—shortly before he died. He was going to show it to Flash and me, but we never made it." Oddly enough, she could now talk about it without her eyes filling with tears. "On the day he died, we were almost there . . ." her voice trailed off. Then she pointed toward the island, smiling. "Look at Flash!"

For a minute, they watched Flash running back and forth, chasing each wave along the beach as it played with the sand. Flash acted like a puppy again.

Then Madeline whispered, "Come on," and she dove from the side of the boat, cutting the water sharply. The cool, soft ripples slid along her body in gentle support as she swam toward shore. Arthur fastened the portable ladder over the rail and followed her.

Neither of them was aware of a misty fog rolling in behind them across the water, nor the white apparition floating tall, just beyond the anchored boat.

They swam for a small cove surrounded on all sides by flat rocks that appeared to form steps. Above those rocks, larger uneven ones nudged the blue sky. They resembled slabs of marble in shades of orange and pink, with tiny white clouds of icing decorating their tops. Everything was so silent, so still. Nothing stirred. Madeline felt as if they had suddenly stepped into one of her mother's paintings.

The beauty of the cove unfolded before their eyes like magic. It wasn't just a visual beauty now, it was a deeper sensation. Madeline felt its power and serenity. There was something mystical about it, almost unworldly and wholly complete. She wondered if Arthur could feel it too.

The next moment, Arthur ran up behind her, breaking the spell. "I'm going to explore!" He grabbed Madeline by the hand. "Come on, let's look around! We'll have to find something to take home—proof that we've been to Sunken Island, something we can find nowhere else in the world!"

Madeline gave Arthur a wide smile. A touch of romance and imagination had taken hold of him. He was beginning to sound like her father. She supposed these were the hidden depths he had promised her at the beginning of the summer. "You go on ahead. I'll be along in a minute."

She stood completely still, yearning to enter the painting once more. The half circle of sand was as white as the clouds, and it sifted like sugar between her toes. Beyond the sand, tall sea grass sprouted, waving beckoning shadows across the rocks. Her father had been right. It was a special island. Pressing her eyes shut hard, she made a wish. Then, as she took a deep breath, she clearly felt her father beside her for an instant. A strong breeze blustered about her, snapping wet hair against her ears. The smell was bold and real, the smell of earth and age, and she tasted salt on her lips. Just above her, feathery clouds wreathed the island, sinking so low she could almost touch them, and she stretched her arms as high above her head as they would go, until her fingertips tingled. The sun was hot on her face, and her eyes were opened wide. Then the breeze faded as quickly as it had come, and only a mild flutter remained, as the clouds drifted upward once more and settled on the rock tops. And her father was gone.

"Madeline! Over here! Look what I've found!" Arthur's voice echoed across the rocks.

Madeline jumped, startled by the reality of a voice. "Where are you?" she called, searching around her. Then, catching sight of his red hair from behind the rocky steps, she hurried in Arthur's direction. "What have you found?" she asked, reaching his side.

"Look at this!" He held up a small sculptured shell, exquisite in detail, a soft-black color. "It's a funny little false-face," he said, turning it over in his hand carefully and examining it. "This is undoubtedly an island of pygmies who dress up for Halloween!" The shell just fit over his hand as he made a fist. "Get the picture?" he laughed.

At once Madeline thought of the swan. It reminded her of a swan's mask. Hesitantly she took the shell, holding it delicately in the palm of her hand. A cold sensation gripped her, and she shuddered.

"What's the matter, Madeline?" Arthur quickly sat down, pulling her down beside him. She dropped the shell. It fell face up, staring at her with two pebbly eyes. "It's only a joke," Arthur went on, putting an arm around her. "Pygmies don't live under water, and I'm sure they've never heard of Halloween." He picked up the shell again. "It belongs to a horseshoe crab or a clam or something like that. It was left behind."

Madeline stared at the shell. It was too perfectly designed to be a discarded shell. It had smooth oval edges and a narrow bridge to fit between two almost oriental eyes. The kind of mask that children wear on Halloween or the harlequin masks that elegant ladies carried to fancy dress balls a long time ago.

Then when the ladies wanted to hide who they were, they held the masks up to their eyes. That was how her mother had described the swans. Swans hid behind masks, too. That's what made them mysterious, her mother had said.

Except there was one swan that didn't wear a mask. That was the swan at the mouth of the harbor, the big swan, the swan that had come at the end of last summer, following the boat on that last sail with her father, and following the boat again today.

She felt dizzy, remembering. The next thing she knew, Flash was licking her face and whimpering anxiously. She hugged him tightly. "It's all right. I'm all right." She turned to Arthur, who knelt over her, a disturbed look on his face. "What happened?"

"I don't know," Arthur answered gently. "But the shell upset you, so I put it back where I found it. Okay?"

"I'm sorry, Arthur." She took hold of his hand and pulled herself up. "I guess all the sun this afternoon finally got to me!"

The water had begun to erase the beach, and the tall sea grass, which earlier had swayed in fresh, lush thickets, was now dried crisp by the sun. It rustled, irritatedly, in the air. The sand was no longer white and it felt coarse now. Even the rocks had taken on a drab, parched appearance. The painting had faded. The tide had run its schedule, and it was time again for Sunken Island to disappear.

"It's getting late," Arthur said, "and the wind's died down to nothing. We'd better set sail before our kingdom returns to the sea!"

Madeline nodded. Then, quite spontaneously, she kissed Arthur's cheek.

"One last swim!" She called to Flash.

The dog splashed quickly into the water, and Madeline ran after him. She glanced back briefly and saw Arthur sitting cross-legged on the beach, pushing sand around. If Charles could see him now, she thought, building a sand castle!

Her toe slid on something at the water's edge where Flash had been sitting. She reached down and picked it up. It sparkled between her fingers.

"Arthur!" she shouted, running back up the beach. She stopped by his side, marveling at what she saw. "Oh, it's great!" she exclaimed. "Your castle!"

"My lady's palace!" He gestured toward her. "A gift from me!"

Madeline stooped down, scooping up some sand and packing it carefully and firmly around the moat. "Oh, I wish we could take it with us!" Then she remembered: "I did find something to take home, though," and she handed Arthur a smooth crystal marble. "I found it over by Flash. It's just a piece of glass, but it's different, somehow, don't you think? It looks so clear. Will it do?"

"Ah, but yes," Arthur rasped, impersonating an elderly jeweler as he investigated a rare gem, "the eye of the storm. I'll give you a million dollars for it." He put the marble into his pocket. "The eye of the storm is always peaceful and quiet," he commented in a sinister tone, "always clear."

Madeline clapped her hands. "I love it! This way we will always be safe when we sail. Even when chaos rages around us on the high seas,"—she shook her fists in the air—"we will hold the eye of the storm in our hands, and we will have peace!" She gave him a hug. "Oh, Arthur, what fun!"

Then, glancing out toward the boat, she imagined something moving through the gathering mist. It was almost ghostlike. It didn't look like Flash. Quickly, Madeline ran down to the edge of the water. She felt some danger. She had to hurry.

"Flash!" she called, jumping into the waves. The water had fallen into a throbbing pattern, and foamy sediment clouded the surface. Pieces of seaweed stuck to her fingers. She didn't see Flash anywhere as she reached the boat, and the mist that encircled her was strangely illuminated, casting an eerie glow around *The Lady.*

"Flash! Where are you?" she shouted, edging herself along the railing toward the bow. Her fingers were numb, and they ached. "Flash! Come here!

We're going home!" She cried in panic, while mouthfuls of salt water choked her cries and stung her tongue. Grimly she forced herself to keep moving along the railing. As she rounded the bow at last, something stopped her. Her eyes felt swollen when she squinted, and her long hair was loose and streaming down her face. Her heart was pounding so hard it seemed to churn the water around her, and the gasps and pantings from the very bottom of her throat made her whole body twist in pain. With almost desperate strength she jerked her head back, and then she saw it—the huge swan, like a great mutant—directly in front of her. "Go away! Go away!" she screamed. "Get out of here!" and she beat the water with her fists until she thought they would break. "Leave us alone! Go away!" She was choking on her screams. "Flash! Flash!"

Then, in calm response, Flash swam past the swan and reached her side. Madeline grabbed his collar, clutching it tightly. "Go away!" she screamed again at the swan. "Go away." Her cries bubbled and drowned in the water.

But the swan hesitated, and Madeline was drawn to look into its eyes. She was spellbound. Deep within those eyes she felt a patience and tranquility that was ageless and supreme. She realized peace at last, and was silent.

Finally, the swan turned and glided away.

Shaken, Madeline scrambled up the ladder and

leaned over to help Flash who climbed aboard easily. "Stay!" she commanded him. "I'll be right back." And this time as she dove back into the water, she felt safe in leaving him.

Arthur had started splashing his way toward the boat when Madeline reached him. "Arthur," she gulped, pulling herself past him to the shore, "wait." The water was chilly now, and the air had turned cold. She was shivering. "I need the eye of the storm."

Arthur reached deep down into his pocket and handed the marble to Madeline. "What happened?" he asked. "What's going on?"

"I'll only be a minute," she called, running toward the sand castle. The tide had reached the edges of the fortress and had begun to trickle through the moat. Madeline pressed the smooth glass into the highest turret of the castle and ran back to Arthur. "The eye of the storm belongs here," she said. "We shouldn't take it away."

They swam out to the boat together. Arthur climbed aboard first, then helped Madeline up the ladder. She was so tired, and, when she finally made it over the rail, she sank down to sit on the floorboards, holding Flash.

"What *happened?*" Arthur asked again as he pulled up the anchor and set sail. "What was all the excitement I missed out here?"

"I'll explain it later," Madeline told him.

The sun was slipping down the sky before them in a dazzling departure of rainbow hues. They were surrounded by luminous colors on all sides. Madeline had never known the heavens to seem so near. Behind them, Sunken Island was slipping once again into the sea.

The wind was sharp, and the air was clear. There was no more fog.

Madeline was suddenly no longer afraid. She was ready to greet the swan, whom she knew could be waiting for their return.

THE END OF
SUMMER

NOW, at summer's end, Madeline and her mother began once more to collect cartons from Mr. Robinson for packing things to return to the city. Boxes once more choked the front hall of the summer house, and a certain quiet expanded.

Charles and Lisa had left a few days before to return to France, leaving Aunt Ede in a slump of welcome solitude.

"You never realize how much you've missed yourself," Aunt Ede was saying to Madeline's mother as the three of them were tying up boxes, "until you're finally alone again, and you've got all that thinking with yourself to catch up on."

Madeline looked up. She had never thought of Aunt Ede as much of a thinker. Aunt Ede was more of a doer—at least, when Madeline was around her in the summertime. She guessed Aunt Ede, too, had hidden depths.

"I wonder," Madeline said, almost to herself, "I wonder if some day we might just stay here. I mean, leave the apartment in the city and just move here for always."

Aunt Ede and her mother stopped work and looked at her. Madeline hadn't really expected an answer, but her mother spoke: "I don't know, Mad. Why? Would you want to?"

"I'm not sure. Maybe. I have friends here." Madeline thought for a moment. "But, I guess it wouldn't be the same, would it? It wouldn't be the summer house then. It would just be another house."

"Well, yes, I suppose so," Aunt Ede agreed, closing up the last box.

"And that might spoil things," Madeline went on. "It might not be so special any more."

"I think that's right, Mad," her mother nodded. Then she added, smiling, "And Aunt Ede wouldn't have her thinking time."

Just then Arthur appeared on the porch. He was carrying a bouquet of flowers and a small box.

"Good morning, Arthur," Madeline's mother and Aunt Ede said, almost in unison, as they started out the door. "We'll see you later."

Arthur held the door open for them.

"I'll put your bicycle in the tool shed with the porch furniture," Madeline's mother called.

"Thanks, Mom."

"Can I help with anything?" Arthur asked.

"No thank you, Arthur—unless you and Madeline want to get Flash out of the way. He's hard to work around these days."

Arthur handed Madeline the flowers and followed her mother and Aunt Ede across the driveway. Madeline noticed with interest the small box going into his pocket.

In a moment, he came back into the house carrying Flash in his arms. Madeline had to laugh. Arthur was a mountain of fur, with a cap of red hair. "You look like the abominable something!" Madeline giggled.

Arthur knelt down, placing Flash gently on the rug. Flash looked much thinner, and the golden retriever now had a lot of gray hair. "How are you ever going to get this dog back to the city?" Arthur asked earnestly. Flash could hardly wag his tail. "I don't think he'll make it."

"He won't have to," Madeline answered. Her voice was solemn, but not sad. "Remember last week, when we came back from Sunken Island, I told you I'd explain something?"

"Yes, I remember."

She took Arthur's hand, and they walked over and sat down on the couch. "Well, it may sound complicated, but it isn't really." She told Arthur about her father and the swan. "The swan is special somehow. It was special for my father, and it's special for Flash now." She frowned a little, trying hard to sort it all out in her own mind. "The swan seems to take care of things and makes going away not so bad. Oh, I don't know," she said, smiling quickly, "it's just a feeling I have, but it's very real."

Arthur put his arm around her, and the two of them sat and talked for a long time. Madeline was amazed at how easy it was to talk to Arthur now, and how easy it was not to cry. "Do you believe that when people die they can take care of the other people who are left behind?" she asked him.

Arthur contemplated the question for a few moments. "Yes, I think so. Your father's done a pretty good job for you this summer."

"What do you think it's like there—I mean, in heaven? When I went to Sunday school, the teachers always said that it was nice and beautiful and people lived there forever, just like they do here, only without any troubles. Do you think that's true?"

Arthur scratched his head slowly. "Heaven is what you want it to be," he answered thoughtfully. "And where you want it to be. And when you want it to be."

"Like right now?" Madeline asked. "Right here in the house by the water, at the end of summer?"

"Why not? If that is what my lady desires!" He

reached down into his pocket and handed Madeline the small box.

She opened it with excitement. Inside there was a small silver sailboat to wear as a charm. Across one side in tiny letters it read THE LADY. And across the other side was inscribed FROM HER CREW.

Madeline's eyes filled with tears, and a lump settled in her throat. "Oh, Arthur, thank you." Her voice was trembling. "Thank you so much."

Arthur pulled her toward him, kissing her gently on the lips. "I'll be going into the city a lot this year," he said, "and I'll be seeing you." He stood up. Tears were streaming down Madeline's face, and she couldn't say a word. She didn't watch Arthur as he left the house and disappeared down the beach, but she did feel Flash press heavily against her side. Hugging him very hard, she could feel his bones. They seemed too fragile.

"It's all right, Flash. Good Flash. It's all right now." Flash followed her slowly as they walked out of the house. Madeline noticed that he was limping. She wished there was more that she could do to help him besides just letting go.

Madeline and her mother spent the rest of the afternoon sealing up boxes and packing the car. Tory and Lee came for a few minutes to say good-bye, and Mrs. Robinson came just after lunch to collect the few remaining vegetables from the garden.

"We had a real good crop this year—especially

the beans," Mrs. Robinson noted. "Your dad would have been proud of us."

Mrs. Robinson took credit for the vegetable garden, and indeed she should have. There just wasn't enough time in Madeline's busy schedule this summer to do all the weeding and spraying, and it didn't seem important to her anymore, without her father. Mrs. Robinson insisted that she would come over and tend to things. Madeline supposed it was Mrs. Robinson's memorial to her father.

"We'll be leaving the first thing tomorrow," Madeline's mother told Mrs. Robinson as they walked over to the delivery truck. "I'll leave the key in the usual place above the door. Any time Mr. Robinson wants to close the shutters and stuff up the chimney is fine with us."

Mrs. Robinson bounded up onto the high driver's seat. She looked so small to handle such a clumsy, big van like that, Madeline thought.

"Good—bye, dear!" Mrs. Robinson called to Madeline. "We're going to leave that picture of you and Arthur up all winter long!"

"Bye, Mrs. Robinson!" Madeline called back, blowing her a kiss. "See you early next summer!"

All that remained to be done was to say good-bye to Aunt Ede and make a final check on *The Lady* and *Banana Peel,* who would spend the winter side by side in the Yacht Club storage space at the farthest end of the parking lot. Madeline and Arthur had sailed *The Lady* to the club the day before, and after hoisting her out of the water, they had given her a protective coat of wax and readied her for the months ahead. Madeline had to check the canvas covers now and make sure they were both tied down securely.

"Ready, Madeline?" her mother asked, as she left the house for the car.

"I just have to get the sails, Mom. Could you please help me carry them out? I'm going to keep all the sails together in the sail loft at the Club."

"Whatever happened to the good old sail bag?" her mother said with a laugh as they struggled into the car with long, stiff tunnels of sails.

"Careful, Mom. We can't bend them. It took Arthur an hour to roll them, and he gave me strict instructions." She smiled, shaking her finger. "Come on, Flash. Your turn," and she lifted him into the car, beside the sails. Flash lay his head down right in the middle of the mainsail, forcing wrinkles down the tube, but Madeline didn't seem to notice.

They drove past the village green, which didn't look too green any longer.

"Do you realize, Mad," her mother observed, "there really wasn't any bad weather this summer. I mean, *really* bad weather, like some other years. It was a good summer."

"Look at Mrs. Chapman's roses." Madeline

laughed. "They look exhausted." Mounds of yellow roses heaped and tumbled over and over one another as they gripped and fell along the picket fence. "I guess Mrs. Chapman just gave up this summer. She couldn't stop them!"

Simpson's house had had a new coat of paint, and the widow's walk sparkled in the late afternoon sun. It would be the time of day when the ladies would have gone down to the sitting room for tea and cakes. Later, probably at dusk, they would return once again to stare out to sea, hoping to catch some glimpse of a ship's lantern returning to safety.

"Some day I'd love to own that house," Madeline said out loud.

Her mother sounded surprised. "The Simpson place? Nobody wants a big house like that anymore."

"I do," Madeline said, with conviction. She suddenly felt very sorry for the big house that nobody wanted, and she felt bad for all the wonderful ghosts she was sure lived there still.

It was good to have a ghost in a house, a ghost who had lived in a house and loved it as much as you did, a ghost who would take care of the house when you had to be away, keeping it safe until you came back, when the ghost would welcome you and keep *you* safe.

They reached the Yacht Club just as Mrs. Davis was pulling out of the parking lot. She slammed on the brakes and her little sports car skidded on the gravel.

"Hi, Madeline!" Mrs. Davis quickly opened the door and wedged herself out of the seat. The car sighed.

Madeline smiled to herself. Little Mrs. Robinson, practically lost behind the wheel of a big truck, and enormous Mrs. Davis squeezed into a little convertible.

"Hi, Mrs. Davis . I haven't seen you all summer."

Mrs. Davis kissed Madeline and her mother. "I've been away looking after my father, but I heard all about the regatta." She nodded to Madeline. "Congratulations!" She clapped her hands, and her straw hat bounced on her head. "By the way, whatever happened about a new boat—the one for you and Flash? Did you find it?"

"Oh, yes, Mrs. Davis. We sure did," Madeline exclaimed. "Right there at Sasco Hill. Just like you said. The same one you told me about."

Mrs. Davis boomed her approval. *"The Lady?* Where is she?"

They parked the cars, and Madeline jumped out. "Come with me!" She took Mrs. Davis by the hand, and Mrs. Davis jiggled along beside her. "Right over here!" Madeline extended her arms and bowed toward the boats, high up on their trailers.

"Two winners together!" Mrs. Davis cried, clapping her hands again.

Madeline thought how much bigger the boats looked out of the water—how grand.

"Is *The Lady* as good a sailor as her old lady?" Mrs. Davis asked.

Madeline nodded. "Flash and I think she's even better," she said with a smile, "because she gets where she's going." Madeline patted both boats on their bows.

They walked back to the car. Mrs. Davis leaned heavily in through the window and gave her mother a good-bye kiss. "You two have a good winter. Take good care of them, Flash." Flash sighed sleepily. "God bless you all! I'll see you next summer!" And she waddled back to her car, wedging herself behind the wheel as she skidded away.

Madeline's mother started the car and backed out of the parking lot. "The boats are in a good spot back there," her mother said, "all alone and safe."

Madeline was pleased also. "Nobody will bother them, and they won't have to get up for the other boats to pass. They both will have a good rest."

"And well deserved. Amen," her mother chimed.

The summer house too seemed to be settling in for a rest. The flower garden had gone to bed, with weeds popping up through the mulch and creeping across the edging like a blanket. Madeline's mother had allowed the flowers to go to seed over the last two weeks, mainly because she had several paintings to finish. Each fall she was expected to exhibit paintings in one of the important city galleries, and her summer's work had always been her major subject. This year, however, Madeline thought her mother's paintings were somehow different. They seemed more somber—none of the usual high, bright colors. A certain childlike boldness was missing. Madeline expected that the gallery might be disappointed with them.

"Maybe my painting has just matured," her mother had suggested.

There's that word again, Madeline thought, but now she understood what it meant. And she liked the sound of it.

"Where's the swan painting, Mom? It's not with the others."

"I thought I'd leave it here, Mad."

"But I really think it's the best one," Madeline said emphatically, as she fingered through the canvases. "These others seem so dark, so different from what you usually do."

Her mother forced a smile. "I guess I matured into my dark period."

She looked very pale to Madeline and very tired. And there was a deep sadness still behind her eyes. Madeline reached over and put her arm around her mother. "I'm sorry, Mom. I wasn't much help this summer, was I? I was always too busy. I never thought much about how you must be feeling—

being here alone all the time. Really, I'm very sorry, Mom." She wanted to add: Thank you very much. Thank you for forcing me to grow up a little, for making me face things, and for pushing me away when you probably needed me the most. Instead, she simply said, "Thank you for the summer."

Her mother smiled easily and gave Madeline an affectionate squeeze. "Let's go buy some hamburgers, bring them home, and have a farewell supper. I'll go get Aunt Ede."

"Great idea!" Madeline cried. "I'll go find Flash!"

Madeline looked everywhere, but Flash was nowhere to be found in the house or in the yard.

Several clouds had suddenly appeared in the sky, making ominous patterns above the water. The waves shivered expectantly. "Flash!" Madeline called again. How could he get to the beach, she wondered. Could he get over the sea wall by himself? He could barely walk.

Nevertheless, she climbed up on the sea wall for a better view. Then she saw the swan near the mouth of the harbor, in the tall reeds. She was surprised only that the swan was alone. Where could Flash be? She jumped down and ran to the water. Thunder growled in the distance. He must be somewhere out there. She called him again. Then, with relief, she saw him swimming toward her. She stared at him in wonderment for a moment.

"Flash! Over here!" she called. "I'm over here!"

The dog emerged from the water, shaking himself

and wagging his tail. In a second he was at her side. She gave him a hug. There was no time for questions. "Come on, Flash. Beat you to the house." It had started to rain, and the thunder grew closer. "Come on! Hurry!" They raced to the house. It was just like old times. As they jumped on the porch, lightning slashed the heavy sky, followed by a deafening explosion of noise. A torrent of rain struck the ground. Madeline pulled Flash inside the door and quickly slammed it shut. Flash huddled down, as if to comfort her. "Flash will take care of us." She remembered telling her father that a long time ago. "Flash will take care of us." She repeated it to herself. But now it was different. She knew the time had come. Flash had always taken care of her. But now he must go.

The rain continued, cool and unyielding. Aunt Ede and her mother had left for the village to pick up the hamburgers while Madeline set the table. She made sure Flash stayed close to her side at every turn. Finally, the two of them went into her father's study to wait. When Madeline opened the door, she saw the painting of the swan over the fireplace.

"So that's where it is! Mom's right. It does belong here." She stood looking at the painting with great appreciation. "I love it more than anything she has ever painted. And it will always belong in this room." She glanced around at the citations and awards on the walls and all the photographs in silver frames.

Suddenly she remembered something she had left in Aunt Ede's car weeks ago, the day that Charles and Lisa had arrived for the summer. She remembered the picture that Lisa had taken of Madeline and her father and Flash on the deck of *The Great Lady*—that day at the end of last summer. Madeline opened the study door in a hurry, hoping Aunt Ede's car was still in the driveway. The rain was slackening as the day ended. Good. They had taken her mother's car to the village. She opened the glove compartment, and there in the very back she found the photograph in the silver frame. She took it out and studied it for a long time. Then she carried it lovingly back to the house. "Flash!" she called. "Come see something!"

Then she noticed that the door had been left open, and the dog had gone. She raced around to the front yard.

In the distance, she could see Flash. He was standing on the sea wall. The rain had almost stopped, and a hazy mist hung lazily in the air as the moon slid into view. "Flash! Come down from there," she called urgently, running across the lawn. "Come! Hurry! I've something to show you!" She pressed the photograph against her heart.

The dog ran toward her, his tail wagging in excitement. He no longer limped. He acted like a puppy again, the way he had acted that day on Sunken Island. Madeline grabbed him, and the photograph fell to the grass. She held him for a long time. There was a strength in him that she had not felt before as he sat patiently, not moving, until finally she let him go. He licked her face. Abruptly, Madeline stood up and brushed away tears. She picked up the silver frame, drying it carefully against her shirt. "Come on, Flash!" she called, and the words caught in her throat. "Beat you to the house!"

She ran as fast as she could to the front door. When she looked around, Flash was nowhere in sight. She called him once, out of habit, but she knew that he would not come.

Then she turned, ran into the house, and hurried to the window at the top of the stairs. She squinted her eyes hard in order to see through the darkness.

There, following a moonbeam path across the Sound, she saw the swan clearly. Its long white neck was bending low again, making a graceful arc into the water beside it. She knew who it was, and she knew it was not alone. There was no reason to be frightened any more, and she knew, in time, the sorrow would fade. Everything would be all right. They would always be with her—her father and Flash.

She would tell the whole story to her mother the next morning on the drive back to the city. And she and her mother would talk about it again and again.

Finally the swan grew very tiny way off in the distance, then rose swiftly into the sky.

About the Author

ANN BROPHY attended Skidmore College and received her B.A. in English literature and creative writing from Western College for Women, Oxford, Ohio. After attending the Katherine Gibbs School in New York, Mrs. Brophy worked with four Broadway playwrights and a syndicated cartoonist.

Mrs. Brophy, who is a member of the Society of Children's Book Writers and The National Writers Club, lives in Southport, Connecticut, with her husband, Charles, and their three children, Anthony, Ruth Ann, and Andrew. FLASH AND THE SWAN is Ann Brophy's first book for young readers.

Tempo Classics

☐ 17150	**JUNGLE BOOK** Rudyard Kipling	$1.50
☐ 16974	**KIDNAPPED** Robert Louis Stevenson	$1.95
☐ 17256	**LITTLE WOMEN** Louisa May Alcott	$2.25
☐ 16069	**PETER PAN** J. M. Barrie	$1.25
☐ 17238	**REBECCA OF SUNNYBOOK FARM** Kate Douglas Wiggin $1.75	
☐ 17148	**THE SWISS FAMILY ROBINSON** Johann Wyss $1.50	
☐ 17136	**TOM SAWYER** Samuel Clemens	$1.50
☐ 17121	**TREASURE ISLAND** Robert Lewis Stevenson $1.50	
☐ 17188	**THE WIND IN THE WILLOWS** Kenneth Grahame $1.50	
☐ 17134	**THE WIZARD OF OZ** L. Frank Baum	$1.50

Available wherever paperbacks are sold or use this coupon.

ACE TEMPO BOOKS
P.O. Box 400, Kirkwood, N.Y. 13795

Please send me the titles checked above. I enclose $_____.
Include $1.00 per copy for postage and handling. Send check or
money order only. New York State residents please add sales tax.

NAME_____

ADDRESS_____

CITY_____STATE_____ZIP_____

T-01